VENDETTA

AN ADULT NOVEL BY

JENNIFER MOULTON

To Randi,

I hope you enjoy my story!

♡ Jennifer Moulton

For my loving, supportive, and wonderfully patient husband, Josh, and my children; Gabriel, J.J. and lily belle.

Thank you to all my friends and family.

I appreciate you all.

R.I.P my dear friend

Allie V.

Edited by Leila Kerschensteiner

PROLOGUE

FROM THE BEGINNING

The sudden slamming of the screen door woke me up. I could hear my sister, Alice, carrying on about something. It probably had something to do with her boyfriend, Joey… again. I rolled over in my bed and squinted, trying to get my eyes to focus on the old clock radio. It was 5:32 p.m. Only another hour and a half until I had to get Lily from the sitters.

"Look! I already said, NO! Okay? So get lost already, I have nothing more to say to you!" Alice yelled.

"So much for getting some sleep around here," I grumbled.

I sat up slowly and stretched, smoothing my hair back. I hadn't been home long. I just worked 36 hours straight on a narcotics case with the Hoboken Police Department.

I stood and pulled my jeans on as I tried to listen to the commotion outside. "They're at it again," I thought.

Yawning and scratching my head, I slowly made my way down the stairs to the kitchen. That's when I heard Alice scream. I scrambled to the window that was facing the alley. I could see my little sister being held by her arm by somebody, but wasn't Joey. It looked like his brother Leo and his two friends, Tommy and

Johnny… whatever their last name was.

I ran barefoot out of the house, heading out to the alley. The sun was setting and it was getting dark real quick on that side of the house. The only light back there was from a lamp post, half a block down. I squinted through the spitting rain as I jogged out there. I could make out three dark haired men and my sister, standing by the dumpsters. Whatever started this stupid argument, I didn't fucking care. I was going to end it. I was in a pissy mood, what do you want? They woke me up.

"Alice, get in the house," I said sternly. "What's going on here?" The other two guys hung back. They shrugged their shoulders and looked confused, like they didn't even know what was going on. The rain started to come down real good now. As usual, Alice didn't listen to me. She stood back though, to see what I might do.

Leo faced off with me.

"Well, if it isn't your big brother, Vinny, the bad-ass cop!" snorted Leo.

"Where's that shiny badge of yours and your fancy gun, Officer Lentini?" Leo asked snidely.

Leonardo Vanzetti. He was an arrogant little prick but, I stood my ground and smiled at him. He didn't intimidate me in the slightest.

"I don't need it tonight, Leo," I said calmly. "I'm not working right now. They're in the house, safe and sound, but thanks for your concern though," I said sarcastically.

"Alice, come here," I gestured for her and she ran to me.

"Look Leo, I know my sister broke up with your brother this morning and for her own good too, but I'll tell you this one time and one time only... harassing her like this and grabbing her arm like that is only going to bring trouble for you," I pointed at him and stared him down.

"Trouble? What kind of trouble, Vin? What you going to do, you're not working tonight, remember? Oh wait, I know... call for back up," Leo and his buddies laughed.

I shook my head. "No, Leo, I can handle you all on my own," I smiled.

"Oh, you think so?" he chuckled. "You can handle me, huh? We'll see about that," Leo said loudly.

He quickly reached up into his jacket and pulled out a gun. I instinctively moved back and Alice screamed. He then pointed it straight at her. I quickly moved in front of her, keeping myself in between them.

"What you going do about this, Vin?" Leo asked amused.

"What are you going to do with that gun?" I calmly asked. "If you want to challenge me, it's got to be a fair fight. Man to man," I stated.

"Leo! Put the fucking gun away," warned Tommy, "We got

no part in this, Vinny," he pleaded. "I swear to fucking God," he said sincerely.

"Leo, man… sorry, but we're gone!" Tommy slowly backed up and whispered, "Sorry, Alice," Tommy took off after his brother. Johnny was already halfway down the alley.

Leo didn't seem to care about what was happening with his friends, nor did he look. His eyes were dark and strangely focused on me. I noticed that he looked like he hadn't slept in a while.

"Why don't you put it away and talk to me man," I said calmly, "You know I'm not packing," I said truthfully.

I lifted up both of my arms. It was obvious that I only had on a pair of jeans. They hung down slightly past my boxers with my belt barely buckled. "How is that gun, going to solve anything that's going on with you right now? Think about that," I said calmly.

"I have been thinking. I've been thinking all day actually, about your sister. She finally broke up with my brother. I thought that maybe she'd realized that I'm the right man for her, not Joey, my punk ass little brother!" He started pacing. He looked at the ground, but the gun was still on us.

"But NO!" He shouted, regaining focus of his thoughts, "She rejected me, too!"

He started to rub at his forehead with his gun hand, clamping his eyes shut like he was grimacing from some kind of physical pain.

I thought this might be my chance to try and get the gun. I took a step closer, trying to slowly bridge the gap between us.

His eyes suddenly shot open and he steadied his hand, "She won't even give me a chance to show her!" He cried out.

"I bet, that if you put the gun away, Leo, we could talk things out; all of us. We're all a little soaked here, you know?" I tried to reason with him. "Guns don't solve problems, Leo. It's only going to complicate things," I said honestly.

"I don't need to talk to YOU, about shit! This is between me and Alice!"

"You had your chance to say what you needed to say to her, and you got your answer, whether you liked it or not. I'm not going anywhere without my sister. I'm sure as hell not going to leave her alone with you, with a fucking gun in your hand!" I was beyond reasoning with him now. It was getting harder to mask my anger.

Looking around me at Alice, he began pleading with her. "Joey's not in the picture anymore, right? You broke things off with him for good now? You guys were always fighting anyway, and he obviously didn't make you happy," his thick Jersey accent was sounding desperate. "Then why not go with me, huh? Why not give ME a chance, Alice? Please? Let me show you that I can be a good guy." Leo begged her.

Alice stayed hidden behind me. I could feel her hand clutching my belt and her warm forehead pressed against the middle of my back.

"I already told you, Leo. I'm still in love with Joey and I don't know why we fight so much," she answered insistently. "It's complicated and really none of your business anyway!" Her breathe was short and ragged. She was shivering.

"What? That makes no sense!" Leo looked shocked, almost betrayed as he staggered backwards towards the fence. "But, he makes you so unhappy, and then when I offer you happiness, you tell me you still want him?" he wept. Leo's injured pride and broken heart was painfully obvious.

From a short distance down the alley, I could hear the clomping of boots sloshing in the rain.

Someone was running towards us. I saw his black leather jacket, wet and glistening in the lamplight. Leo looked to his left at the shadow approaching. I stiffened up preparing to tackle him for the gun, when I heard Joey, yell out…

"Leo! What the hell you think you're doing?" Joey stopped running and swiftly walked up behind his brother. "Tommy and Johnny came over to the restaurant and - " his voice trailed off mid-sentence when he saw Alice crouching behind me. "Alice, are you okay?" Joey looked legitimately concerned.

Alice screeched out a warning, "He's got a gun Joey, be careful," her face was still pressed into my back.

Joey's gaze shifted back to Leo. Suddenly, realizing the intensity of the situation, he stood still.

Joey changed his tone and decided to try and talk to him.

"Leo, what's going on with you, bro? Please, just put the gun away before someone gets hurt, huh?" Joey said to him.

Leo snorted loudly, as pushed his shoulders back. He slowly moved to his left, inching closer to his brother. Joey, wanting to keep his distance from Leo now, moved towards us. I pivoted to keep Alice behind me. Then I realized what Leo was doing… he was herding us together.

He strutted nervously now, as he prepared to make his point.

"She goes around acting like she's too good for you all the time! I can see why you fight now," he laughed nervously. He pointed the gun in our direction, shaking it at us as he spoke. "This stupid cop's precious, little sister is apparently too good for anyone in our dirty, little crime family," he laughed.

"What are you talking about, Leo?" Joey was confused. He'd obviously missed something.

Alice's shaky little voice came out from behind me in a shock. "He made a move on me Joey," she exclaimed, "I turned him down… I told him that I was still in love with you!"

I reached behind to shush her, as if to say, "Shut up, this isn't helping, Alice." She nodded her head in silent agreement and swallowed hard.

Joey quickly stepped forward, glaring at Leo. Joey's face twisted in anger. "I get into an argument with MY girl and you get your fuckin' cronies to come down here with you to harass her at her home? Not to mention, see what's in it for you?" Joey was rocking back and forth, clenching his jaw as he spoke.

He continued. "You're classy, brother! You know, when Tommy came into the restaurant and told me you were starting shit with the cop, I didn't expect this," he smirked. "Never in my life, would I believe you could be as low as scum."

"You're fucking psycho, if you think she would ever want someone like you!" Joey leaned in closer, "You-don't-know- a-thing, about me and Alice!" Joey glared into Leo's face, "So now you've decided to pull a gun on the woman I love and her family? You're certifiable!" Joey got up close and stared long and hard into his stunned brother's eyes… and spit.

Leo roared with anger as he shoved the barrel of the gun into Joey's chest, pushing him back.

"Are you going to shoot me ...   BROTHER?" Joey yelled.

Leo bit down hard on his lower lip, drawing blood. His hand was constantly slicking the water off of his oily black hair. His shifty eyes were glancing at everyone. Leo was panicking.

"Shut your mouth, you little punk! I'm the one in control right now, not you!" He growled.

Alice got as close to me as she could. She buried her head into my back and grabbed my waist. I could feel her shiver and shake.

"Yeah, okay, you're in control Leo..." Joey laughed. He

slowly stepped in front of me. "But this is what's ACTUALLY going to happen. Vinny's gonna to get Alice inside where it's warm and dry.

He's gonna to move real slow… aren't you Vinny?" Joey kept his eyes on Leo.

"That's right," I answered him.

"Thank you, Vinny. It's not good for Alice… or the baby, to be out here in this cold rain," he smiled slyly, purposefully revealing Alice's secret.

The expression on Leo's face, matched mine.

I was speechless. "What baby?" I thought.

"A baby?" Leo managed to squeak out the actual word.

Alice tensed up as she sucked in a breath. I looked at Joey who was confidently staring down Leo. The gun was still pointed at him. I spun around to look at Alice, my eyes wide with disbelief as I searched her cherub face for an answer. Her eyes were closed and her lips were trembling.

"I'm sorry Vin! I was gonna to tell you tonight. I just found out this morning and I haven't had a chance to figure out how to say it yet!" She started crying so hysterically, she stumbled over every word. Her brown curls were wet and matted, sticking to her tear drenched face.

"Shhh… it's okay! Everything's gonna be okay. I love you,

no matter what and you're gonna to be alright." I smoothed the hair out of her face. Her beautiful, hazel eyes looked up at me with uncertainty, as she wrapped her arms around me and squeezed. Her little body, now seemingly fragile, shivered as she buried her face in my chest. I put my arms around her instinctively to steady her. I needed to protect my little sister. That was it for me. No more games, I needed to diffuse the situation, immediately.

"Joey, come and get Alice," I ordered. "You've played the jealousy game long enough." Alice looked up at me, startled. "What are you doing," silently entered my thoughts. "Don't worry," I whispered.

Joey snorted and quickly took Alice into his arms as I turned to size up Leo's current mental state. He had to be fuming with anger. Shouldn't he? But, instead, his face was completely void of all emotion. He just stood still, frozen in time. The gun was now hanging at his side. Thank God.

"Leo," I said quietly. "The situation has changed, don't you think? Maybe we could rethink things a bit." I was directly in front of him now. His eyes were pinned, staring at the ground, and his hand was shaking. The rest of his body was stoic.

"I think we were both a little shocked by the sudden baby news. Some things are starting to make a little more sense now, don't you agree?" He didn't respond. "I know that deep down you care about your brother. Your relationship is all complicated right now, but you'll get past this. Those kids will work out their issues, they always do... in their own way." Still, no change.

"We can all get past this and pretend like this incident never happened. I will completely forget that you ever came here tonight. So just relax and give me the gun Leo, it's all over now." I slowly took a step forward.

Leo's body reacted and flew back, as if I had hit him. His dark brown eyes flashed at mine with a newfound rage. The hair on my neck stood straight up.

"Shut the fuck up, already!" He screamed, "I can't just act like nothing ever happened, because it did!"

He franticly shook as he aimed the gun right at my face. I raised my left hand, as a sign of surrender. With my right, I began pointing towards the house, repeatedly, gesturing for Joey and Alice to get going.

"You stupid idiot!" shouted Joey. "Would you stop and realize what he's trying to say to you? He's trying to help you! Why don't we let Vinny take Alice inside and you and I settle this, huh?" Joey taunted his older brother, again. "We got some unfinished business, don't we, brother?"

Leo looked like a wounded child.

"You care more about protecting that broad, than me! What about our relationship? What, you don't want to be my brother anymore?" Leo was weeping once more.

"Ugh! You're so screwed up in the head, bro! Who's got a gun pulled, huh? What did you do, eat a fuckin' "eight ball" for dinner?   I know you weren't at the restaurant with pop and me, or with the rest of the family for that matter!" Joey's words added fuel to Leo's fire. The gun shook violently, still pointed at my head.

"So, yeah, of course I'm going to defend my woman and child against a crazy ass, lunatic!" Joey yelled.

Joey had gotten Leo's attention now. I paused and waited for my sign, my "click". It's an unexplainable moment for me, like a switch that flips on inside my brain, instantly telling me the exact time to act.

Leo smirked. "You still want to take her side over mine? Till' death do you part? She doesn't even deserve to have a Vanzetti child! She's just a stupid whore!"

CLICK.

I slammed into Leo with all of my body weight, taking him down to the gritty asphalt. I grabbed at his gun arm on the way down. I grappled a hold of it, but I couldn't get a firm grip with my slippery hands. He rolled me onto my bare back trying to wrestle his arm from my grasp. I had a partial hold on the gun barrel, but my hand slipped off again. I desperately held on to his arm and wrist, tearing up his sleeves. I kneed his back and elbowed his kidneys, trying anything to subdue him. I pushed off the ground with my feet and back, heaving his body up off of mine. I flipped him over on his side, lunging over him, grappling for his gun hand. He punched my back with his free hand. Something about it didn't feel right. I almost had the gun in my control when I felt a seething, sharp pain in my side. It twisted and released, twice. I knew then he wasn't punching me at all. He was stabbing me, repeatedly. Warm blood trickled down my side.

Alice was screaming something to me, but I couldn't make out the words. Joey had grabbed her and was attempting to run down the alley. He struggled to hang on to her, but she was yanking her body in the opposite direction, trying to get back to me.

"Run Alice, get far away! Call 911!! Call Sarge! Get her outta here Joey!" I yelled and screamed until I had no air left inside me, which didn't last long. My lung had collapsed. I held onto Leo as tight as I could. I wasn't going to let him catch up to them. I felt a dull "THUD" as he stabbed my back, as I lay over him. Thud, thud. He rolled me onto my back and I felt the warmth of the blood spreading over my chest and throat. My throat clenched up, causing me to cough, spraying blood over my face and drizzle into my ears. I felt a strong amount of pressure in my eye, before it went dark. Then I realized that the weight of his body had lifted from mine. I was losing consciousness, and could no longer breathe and was too weak to fight anymore.

The sounds of shots fired echoed through the alley way. "Pop! pop, pop, pop!"

I couldn't see anything, only the blurred shadows my brain and damaged eye socket would allow. My eyes were open weren't they? I fought to see. I tried to raise my arms, desperate to go after Leo. They wouldn't move. Was I blinking? All I saw was darkness, and the only thing I could hear, was a loud ringing in my ears.

"Alice," I mouthed the word. My body felt like a cement blanket had been laid over me. I felt myself drifting off to sleep. I was too weak to move anymore. I just needed to hang in there. I just thought of Lily, my daughter. Alice would make it! We all would. We were fighters… we were Lentini's. They had to have gotten away. They had to make it. That's all that mattered right now.

The last thing I remember is the sirens… the echo's in the alley… and then it faded… as quickly as it came.

I awoke to a strange beeping sound. It was extremely annoying. Why can't I ever get any damn sleep? My body was so stiff and my back ached into my hips like I hadn't moved in a week. I suddenly realized that I wasn't familiar with my surroundings. I panicked, because I couldn't see very well. Everything was so blurry. I sensed someone was there, beside me.

I tried to speak. "Who's there? Where am I?"

My lips were cracked. They split even more as I struggled to speak. My tongue was dry, like sand paper, as it licked out to soothe them. I swallowed hard.

"Hey, soldier. It's me, Sarge. You're in the hospital, Vin. You're going to be alright," he reassured me, "Here… have some water," he helped guide my hand to the styrofoam cup he offered. It was full of ice water. I took a small sip. It tasted like rust. I cleared my throat, so I could try to speak again.

"How are you feeling? Do you need the nurse?" I felt him sit down next to me on the bed. He helped me as I struggled to sit up. "Sorry about all the questions," he chuckled, nervously. "I'm just glad you're awake now."

My good eye focused a bit as I rubbed out the crusty bits of blood and mucus. My head ached and my equilibrium was spinning out of control.

"No, it's okay. I just need to find my sea legs," I said dryly.

"Do you remember why you're here?" Sarge asked hesitantly.

"Kind of. There was an argument between Alice, Joey and Leo," I strained to look around the room as I remembered.

"He pulled a gun and I eventually jumped on him. I tried to take it away…but…" I lost my train of thought. I lightly touched the bandages on my head.

 I tried to remember more…but couldn't.

"I'm sorry, man. I'm feeling pretty doped up. Maybe the questioning could wait a few."

"Well, shit. That's more than I expected you to remember. I'm glad your brain still works," he said jokingly.

"I know that you were stabbed multiple times all over your body. They had to do some surgeries on your eye to repair the damage and they had to fix your lung, it had been punctured. You also had a brain hemorrhage and they needed to drill a hole in your head to release pressure and let it drain out properly. You have a couple of broken ribs, but other than that you're all sewn up now and you should be healin' up soon. The Doc will tell you more when he gets in here, that should be any second now," Sarge said.

"Here he comes now, Sir," said an unfamiliar voice coming from the corner of the room.

"Who's that? Is someone else in here?" I asked startled. I couldn't see him.

"Yeah, he's just a rookie I got trainin' wit me today. He tagged along with me this mornin," Sarge said quickly.

"He sounds familiar," I said.

"We'll give you some privacy now, okay?   It's good to see you awake, buddy." Sarge stepped out of the room, but he was holding something back. I recognized the indifference in his voice… even If I did have gauze on one of my eyes, I could see through that.

~

I was sitting up drinking some more ice water when Sarge came back in about an hour later. "Hey, Vin, are you feeling better?"

"Yeah, I'm waiting out this morphine man… I'm a little drowsy, but much more alert than when you left me last." I smiled a half grin, and tried to make out his shadow. I reached over and adjusted the blinds to let in some light. That was better. I could at least see the transition from light to dark.

"Where's Lily? I need to make sure that Alice remembered to pick her up from her play date. Have they been in here to visit at all?" I asked curiously.

"Lily's fine! She's with Trish at our house. She's been stayin' wit us and having a blast with the kids. You've been in here a little over a week, you know," he spoke carefully. Sarge looked down and turned his watch around his wrist. I had a bad feeling knotting up in my stomach. He only did that when he was nervous or anxious about something...

"Vinny, are you up to answering some questions for Detective Rogers?" Sarge quickly changed the subject.

"Rogers? Is he from Homicide?" I asked.

"Yeah, Vin, he is," Sarge said softer.

"Yeah, of course," I said cooperatively. I was sure he needed to get my first hand recollection, maybe even write up a statement about the stabbing, for the attempted murder charges to stick.

"Alright, soldier, you know the drill. Can you tell us what you remember happenin' that night of the… argument?" Sarge asked me.

Detective Rogers interjected. "We should ask him about…"

Sarge stopped him immediately and said "Just write your

damn notes as he tells it! You got it? I'll ask the damn questions," he growled.

"Fine," Rogers responded. I could feel the mounting tension in the room.

I cleared my throat and began. "Leo Vanzetti and two of his friends, Tommy and Johnny, came to the house to talk to Alice. It was about 5:30 or so. They actually woke me up yelling at each other. Alice had previously gotten into an argument with Joey and they had broken up that morning. I looked out the window and saw Leo yelling at her and that's when I saw him grab her arm. I ran out there in nothing but jeans. Leo quickly became erratic and pulled a gun. His buddies took off. Not long after, Joey shows up. Tommy went and told him I guess. I tried to talk him down and shield Alice, the entire time. The two brothers basically began to argue over Alice and then Joey finally told us why Alice was so moody these days!" I chuckled a little. My ribs ached. "He tells Leo that Alice is pregnant with Joey's baby!" I reached over and smacked Sarge's arm, "Can you believe it?" I said excitedly.

Sarge closed his eyes and looked down.

"So, uh, anyways, Leo was apparently high, presumably on methamphetamines, his usual drug of choice, I tackled Leo when I had a chance and sent the kids running down the alley. I knew he was stabbing me; I just didn't want him to get control of that gun till I knew that Alice was long gone. Then I heard shots fired and sirens soon after. I knew then that Alice had called you. That's about it, I mean, other than waking up here," I finished.

A dead silence filled the room.

I heard the loud snap of a briefcase closing. "Ok, that's it, Rogers... you're done here," Sarge stood up and walked over to the door and opened it for him.

Rogers seemed hesitant. "But sir, what about..."

Sarge silenced him. "I said you're done. Now get out and let me talk to my partner!" Sarge hissed.

"Yes sir. Thank you for your time, Vinny. I'm sorry about... everything that happened to you," Detective Rogers got up and walked out quickly.

"Yeah, thanks man. I appreciate it," I said, respectively.

Sarge came back toward the bed. He was rubbing his bald head from front to back.

"Vin, I need to tell you what happened after you blacked out," Sarge sat down at the foot of my bed. He fumbled with his watch again, turning it round and round.

"So tell me, then." That sick feeling returned to my gut.

"I don't know how to start this." He put his head down into his hands, and steadied his feet on the hard hospital floor. "I'm real sorry, Vinny." He took a deep breath...

"Alice and Joey... didn't make it," he exhaled.

I stared at his blurred shape sitting on my bed. They didn't make it? What did that mean exactly?

"Didn't make it where?" I asked.

Sarge continued.

"We received a 911 call from the neighbor. When we heard that it was next to your house, all officers responded that were in the area. We found you first, damn near bleeding to death with the gun at your side. They found Alice and Joey down at the end of the alley…. they were both shot in the back. Leo did a bad job of framing you though. His prints were all over the gun, not to mention all of your blood on his clothes when we found him. He still had the bloody knife folded up in his pocket," he leaned back staring at the ceiling… with tears in his eyes.

I kept listening, hoping that he would say they had made a mistake and that Alice and Joey were fine and recovering in the hospital as well. I tried to make sense out of my own thoughts, but the reality of it had begun set in.

"Leo killed them?" I said. My tears stung at my swollen eyes.

"Yeah, there gone, Vinny. I'm so sorry for your loss," Sarge added. "I didn't know Alice was… with child. That's going to make a difference in court for sure."

"You said you got him?" I asked. My mind was reeling.

"Yeah, we got him. I handled the bastard myself," Sarge cleared his throat.

"We're really gonna to need you to testify in court as to the events of that night. The neighbor won't do it, what with Leo's reputation and all. Leo's family is still connected to the mob and there's a chance that the Vanzetti's might retaliate. We'll protect you and Lily though, don't you worry about any of that. It's gonna to be a witness protection type of deal and you'll definitely need to relocate after you testify; change your names and all that. Don't worry about what's going to happen to Leo, he's going away for a very, long time...." his words trailed off. "I'm so sorry, brother," Sarge lowered his head once again, and sat in silence. I felt his hand squeeze the calf muscle of my leg.

My body went numb. It felt paralyzed. I tried to move my legs. I kicked out and brought them up to my chest. I started to rock back and forth in my bed. I knew my body was physically moving, but I still couldn't feel it. I tried to speak and couldn't make a sound.

A sharp pain shot through my chest. Was it my broken ribs? A roaring, deafening sound filled my ears. I grabbed both sides of my head and leaned back. The sharp pain worsened as my head began to pound. I then realized that the loud groaning sounds were coming from me. A sudden, heavy weight was pushing me down. Sarge had pinned my shoulders down to the bed.

A nurse suddenly appeared at my side with a needle injecting something into my I.V.

My sorrow and sadness had quickly turned into anger and physical pain. It created a rage so white hot with hate... that it was all I could see. It was all I could feel. My mind used that rage to desperately fill the empty hole in my heart that Alice's death had created. I lay in the hospital bed weeping, heavily sedated and unable to grasp my own reality. I incoherently spoke of revenge and dreamed of redemption in the most brutal and merciless of ways. Leo, in my mind, would forever be a killer of innocence and a coward.

Over the next couple of weeks, I would heal physically and endure a mental battle of good versus evil. My only solace was Lily. She was my peace of mind; my "Lily of the Valley" in a land of sadness and despair.

My only glimmer of hope in this sadistic world is my daughter. She was now my only reason to live. With my mother and sister Alice both gone now, I knew I had to do whatever it took to protect what I had left. Sarge knew I would testify, even if we had to start a new life somewhere else. That was the best thing for us anyway. He knew I would do whatever it took to bring down Leo and to create a semblance of justice for my sister and her baby. Even for Joey. I would testify against the world.

Some say that time and time alone can heal all wounds. For mine and Lily's sake, I hope it's at least a little bit true.

CHAPTER 1

13 YEARS LATER

"Bye, Dad!" Allie rushed past Mark and grabbed her heavy back pack off the kitchen counter. She grunted as she heaped the strap up over her shoulder. It amazed him that her string bean, ballerina frame, could lug that thing around like it was nothing.

"Will you be coming home right after school to get ready for your birthday dinner?" He asked, peering over the rim of his coffee cup.

She suddenly stopped fussing with her bag and spun around to face him. She grimaced in hesitation, like she had something to tell him, and didn't know how to start.

He raised his eyebrows. "Inquiring minds want to know."

Her sweet dimpled smile was a bit crooked as she stammered out the details.

"Well, Jen wanted to show me this little coffee shop down

town," she smiled her dad's same goofy grin.

"Do all teenage girls smile when they talk?" He thought to himself.

"So, you think that because you're eighteen now, you can just "ditch out" on your dad any time you want," he said sarcastically.

"It was really a spur of the moment invite and I forgot to tell you about it last night. I'll be home in time for dinner, I promise. I won't be late. Is it alright?" She waited in anticipation.

Mark tried to look serious. "I don't know. Do you have your pepper spray?" He was stalling now.

"Dad," she cocked her head to one side and rolled her eyes. "Nothing's going to happen to me in a coffee shop, in Idaho, in broad day light," she scoffed.

Mark could hear Jens stereo as she pulled into the driveway. Jen was Allie's best friend. "Nearest and dearest," she would say.

"You would be surprised what could happen in broad day light. It's a simple question darling, do you have your pepper spray?" he asked again.

"Yes, Dad, there are two canisters in my backpack and don't forget the stash in my locker at school," she gently grasped her chin and pretended to think really hard. "I'm pretty sure Jen still has an arsenal in her glove compartment," she smiled.

He stood up from the table and walked over to the back door, where she stood. "Alright, be careful and I'll see you sometime after school," he smiled at her as he opened the door.

"Oh, you're so awesome! Thanks for understanding, Dad,"

she hugged him quickly. "I've got to get going now okay, Jen's waiting," she nodded towards the back lot.

"Have a great day at school! Enjoy your coffee for me, huh?" Mark winked at her.

"Oh, school will be a blast, don't you worry," she said sarcastically.

She stopped just short of the door and turned to look up at him through her thick, hooded lashes. She flashed her dimpled smile, and with those big hazel eyes, Mark thought that she looked just like her Aunt Alice.

She hugged him tight, wrapping her arms around his chest to squeeze. He kissed the top of her head.

"Have a great day, Allie-Cat, I love you!" He raised his hand and waved to Jen.

"I love you too, Dad, thanks!" He walked with her out onto the porch and watched as she ran to her friend's car, or whatever you call that thing. It looked like a Jeep, but Jen insisted it was a Samurai.

The girls squealed and giggled in their seats for an excited moment before buckling in. Jen pretended to adjust her mirrors and look extra cautious.

"Silly girls," Mark mumbled to himself.

And that was that. Allie was off to school. Senior year was going to be an exciting time for her.

Mark slowly walked up the creaky, golden stained, wood porch and bent down to pick up the morning paper. Mark went inside and closed the door behind him. He sauntered into the sunlit kitchen and refilled his coffee cup before settling down at the breakfast bar to read. He loved these sunny autumn mornings. "Indian Summer", as Allie calls it.

Mark didn't have to work at the restaurant he managed today. This is very unusual for a dedicated, single father like himself, but even he had to admit… it felt pretty good to just sit and relax, without having anything pressing to deal with. He had every intention of getting ready for the day; just not yet.

You see, today wasn't just any ordinary day. It was Allie's eighteenth birthday party. Angelo's Restaurant was closed today in preparation for it. No catering, deliveries or dining at all to the public. They had been secretly advertising the closure for a week, mostly to the regulars, by word of mouth. Mark didn't think closing the restaurant was necessary, but Dom Angelo, the owner, thought so.

"Allie is my Goddaughter and it's very important to have a big, surprise party for her. Closing the restaurant for it is common sense. Don't you worry so much, Marko" Dom had said.

Mark was Dom's new partner and longtime friend. Dom's wife Lucy, who occasionally worked in the kitchen and as a hostess, was planning and coordinating this special event. She was definitely going to go all out for our princess. Mark was fully aware of her capabilities and never doubted Lucy's party planning abilities for a second. He was blown away by the attention to detail that Lucy was obviously displaying in the decorations. He wouldn't have done a very good job, if left to his own devices.

Allies birthday, technically had passed, but was during a very busy week. All though, they had a small celebration, they had planned to surprise her with this all along.

Silver twinkling lights draped over the ceiling and cascaded down the walls. Garlands of white roses and lilies were arranged nicely and hung over the arched doorways. The sweet fragrance from the fresh, delicate flowers was thick in the air. Rows of rectangular tables were covered with dark purple cloths, and adorned with polished silverware.

Sparkling crystal bowls filled with water had purple and silver floating candles inside them. At the base of each bowl, were a mixture of beautifully arranged white roses and vibrant green ivy. The center pieces were being carefully prepared by many helpers. Mark wasn't recognizing a lot of the extra help that was hired specifically for today. They hadn't hired the usual "extras" from the temp-agency they used occasionally. The flowers, color schemes, and over all style was perfect. It was all Allies favorite colors and flowers. Lucy knows Allie very well, and it shows. That just makes it all the more special for Allie.

"Well, Marko, what do you think so far? Everything's alright?" Lucy asked. She must have seen him gawking. Mark could hear her heels clicking behind him, and her Italian accent was unmistakable.

"Oh, yes Lucy, everything is so beautiful! She's going to love it," Mark said sincerely.

Lucy smiled wide and clapped her hands together. "Wonderful! You must come this way, quickly; I want to show you the cake!" She was already off, clicking away towards the back of the hall.

He walked towards the back of the room and entered the kitchen through the stainless steel double doors. Lucy quickly emptied the room and ordered, "No one is to touch this cake!" she said loudly, commanding everyone in the room. When Lucy spoke, everyone listened whether they wanted to or not.

"Well, this is it, my Masterpiece! What do you think? Do you think she will be pleased?" Lucy looked at me curiously with raised eyebrows.

It was a gorgeous three tiered cake. Extremely detailed with crème colored icing, purple roses and bright green foliage twisting and turning, cascading down the to the bottom tier.

"This is the most lavish birthday cake I've ever seen. Lucy, you have really out done yourself!" Mark was shocked.   "You truly have a gift as a wonderful baker," he said honestly.

"Oh, you're just saying that," she said coyly.

"I mean it, Lucy... it looks like a wedding cake!"

"Thank you, Marko, you're too kind! This is real ivy you know," she pointed out.

"It's amazing what you've done with everything, Lucy, I couldn't have planned all this out in a million years," he laughed.

"I know! Now, leave me, I'm very busy," she grasped his shoulders firmly, almost too hard, as she quickly pecked his cheek, and disappeared through the double doors.

Mark walked back out into the busy dining hall and thought about what Allies' reaction to all of this might be. She was going to love all of this attention; that was for sure! All of her friends will be here, enjoying all her favorite foods. Anybody who knows Allie, KNOWS how she feels about her lamb chops! Mark stood and watched his workers hustling about, politely smiling and nodding at the few who happened to notice him.

"Our little princess is all grown up," Dom's said in his usual deep voice, as he quietly walked up behind Mark.

"Yes, she is, as much as I hate to acknowledge it. The inevitable has happened and way too fast, might I add," Mark admitted.

Dom chuckled. "She will be pleased, no?" Dom gestured to the dining hall.

"She will! She might even be speechless, if you can imagine that!" Mark laughed.

Not joking any longer, Mark turned and spoke directly to Dom.

"I want you to know, that your generosity is greatly appreciated. This will be a big night for her, and very memorable for us all. I thank you and Lucy both; I am truly in your indebted to you," Mark said humbly.

"You're family, Marko. There is no debt to be paid. Stop thanking us, it isn't necessary, as we all know you to be very gracious and sincere. Come, let's discuss business," Dom patted Marks back as they turned towards the hallway.

Stepping aside frequently to stay out of the people's way, they walked down the narrow hall to Dom's office, chatting and addressing finished paper work for incoming shipments next week.

"There's plenty of extra help today," Dom sat down at his desk. "Only Lucy knows what to do, and how to do it, so let's not get in her way!" They laughed. "Everything will go as planned tonight, so don't you worry about a thing." Dom stopped smiling and cleared his throat.

"I would like to address something with you," Dom said.

"Go right ahead," Mark allowed.

"You know how I adore Allie. I want you to know that I will always look after you both, regardless of whatever happens with the restaurant. I have no children and you're the closest I'll ever have to that," Dom looked at Mark very seriously. Mark undoubtedly believed him. Dom was very trustworthy.

Dom always spoke what was on his mind, and this made it especially easy to be his friend as well as a business partner. At least you know where you stand with him, and that's a rarity these days. Mark had a great amount of respect for this man. However, this time there was a subtlety to what Dom was saying. Almost like he was hiding something… and NOT saying what he wanted to. NOT expressing what was really on his mind.

"We feel the same towards you, Lucy, Nick, and Julie... we're all family here," Mark answered cautiously. He wondered where Dom's sudden sentiments were coming from. Was the old man getting soft?

"Dom, you gave a single father a job, with many promotions after and have always treated us like your own. I don't take that for granted and I hope you don't think I do either," Mark said.

"I don't think that at all. Those promotions were given, rightly so," Dom said, as a matter of fact.

Mark nodded in agreement, still perplexed by the odd conversation. He noticed that Dom's expression had become distant as he stared down at his desk top calendar.

Mark hesitated briefly, but decided to say something. "Is everything alright Dom? Is there something else going on here, maybe something with Anita, your sister? I heard she's had difficulty with her Rheumatoid Arthritis," he added.

Dom looked up and stared intensely at Mark for a moment before his dark eyes softened.

"Everything is fine, Marko, don't you worry. Something's just aren't spoken as often as they should be. Yes, my sister has had difficulty getting around since Sophia, my niece has moved out on her own. I will be spending quite some time with her this weekend," Dom stated.

"I'm sorry to hear that. I'm glad she has you to be there for her. Obviously, if there's anything we can do to help you, just let us know," Mark knew Dom would never ask him for help, but he saw how much this bothered him. He had never seen Dom so distracted.

"Thank you, Marko. Again, there's no need to worry," he said smiling.

"Everything will be just fine," Dom assured him.

Mark didn't feel assured at all.

Dom turned and opened a cupboard behind him and took out two wine glasses, placing them on his desk. He reached down and took out an old bottle of wine from his bottom desk drawer. Mark knew that this bottle was saved for a special occasion.

"Now, dear friend," he poured as he spoke, sounding jubilant, "Let's toast! In just a few short hours our princess shall be arriving through the royal doors," he grinned.

Mark relaxed a little as Dom changed the subject. He also realized the sudden truth in Dom's words. Where had the time gone? His day off had flown by. That figured.

They raised their glasses of deep burgundy and swirled it around in their glasses, inhaling the sweet musky aroma.

"To family, and loyalty," Dom declared, making sure their eyes met.

"To family, and loyalty," Mark repeated. They nodded and clinked glasses.

Mark sipped on his glass of red wine, as his mind lingered on their earlier conversation. Mark was certain that there was something odd about it. Mark's intuition beckoned him, but he needed to let it go. He was also certain of one other thing; that was that his daughter was going to have the most memorable night of her life, and he wasn't about to let anything in the world ruin that. Maybe then, she won't be so upset with him if she ever finds out that he paid her best friend to take her out for coffee.

CHAPTER 2

FLOATING CANDLES

Mark was sitting at the kitchen table with his back to the wall, reading the newspaper, when Allie came in through the back door. He asked her how her day was.

"It was good. Well, I was busy at school, but the highlight of the day was the coffee shop! I loved it there, it was so peaceful and cozy," she said happily, "very cool."

He didn't look up at her at all, he just calmly nodded. "Good," he said, "How was their coffee?" he asked.

"Oh, it was amazing! The place is really cool Dad; you'll have to go with me some time… if you're not too old, that is," she looked at him, trying to get a rise out of him. "It might not be your scene," she joked, "but they do have newspapers." He still didn't look up.

She lugged her heavy bag over to the breakfast bar and flung it down on the counter top with a loud thud. Allie peered at her father through squinted eyes.

"Why do I get the feeling I'm about to be in trouble for something that I may or may not have done?" she asked.

He shrugged. "I don't know, are you feeling guilty about something? Why else would you be so suspicious?" Mark grinned.

"Why?" Her eyes widened and she raised her eyebrows. "Because of that smile on your face, that's why!" She coyly grinned.

He slowly revealed a gift box that he was hiding under the table. "Well, I might have a little surprise for you," his twinkling hazel eyes and crooked grin gave it all away.

"Dad," she said surprised. "Oh, my goodness… what's this for? My birthday was almost two weeks ago. What is it?" she asked.

"Well, sit down and open it up… find out for yourself," he gestured to the table and pulled out her chair.

She gently slid off the purple satin ribbon from the long white box and set it aside. "We need to save this," she mentioned.

Allie reached through the crinkly tissue paper and gently pulled it back, revealing her gifts. It was a black, satin dress decorated with sparkling crystals and beads. There was a purple ribbon sache at the waist. Another present was then seen at the bottom of the box. It was a matching pair of shoes of the same color as the ribbon. She sat down, without saying a word. She gently ran her fingers over the smooth satin shoes.

Mark panicked. "Do you like the dress, and slippers? Or flats, whatever they're called. I picked it out myself and you know how I can be..." Mark was afraid he had picked out the wrong style. "Look, I know you're not a little girl anymore, but I couldn't resist, this one.... last time," he gulped, trying to swallow the lump that had formed in his throat.

Allie put her hand on her father's arm to quiet his nervous chatter. She looked up at him... with tears welled up in her eyes. "There beautiful, thank you," she smiled, as the tears blinked down her cheeks. "It's perfect. I'm never going to be too old for your surprises, thank you, Daddy."

"Oh, come here, baby. You're very welcome," he hugged her and kissed the top of her head. "I didn't mean to make you cry, honey," Mark consoled her. He couldn't be more relieved that she liked his gift. Correction; Loved.

"It's ok, Dad, they're happy tears, I just appreciate it. It's very sweet," she said wiping her face.

"Now, I want you to go upstairs and get yourself ready. Put your new duds on, because we're going out to dinner tonight, just you and me," Mark said.

He helped wipe away a runaway tear on her cheek.

"Duds? Really, Dad," Allie joked.

"Yeah, I should've stopped while I was ahead," he smiled. "Okay, run along… tonight's going to be really special!"

Allie grabbed her gift box and stopped at the doorway. She turned and said, "Of course it will be… it'll be with you, Dad, and that's all that matters."

~

Mark guided his daughter into the restaurant wearing a blind fold. He explained that he had one more surprise for her. When he finally took it off, all of the friends and family, who had so patiently waited, jumped up and shouted, "SURPRISE!"

Mark kept his arm around her and walked her to the center of the loud, cheerful room. To say she was surprised would have been the understatement of the year. She was stunned with disbelief.

"What in the world is this? Dad, everybody's here!" she exclaimed.

"Happy belated-birthday, honey," he whispered excitedly to her. She mouthed the words "thank you," as she was led away by her excited friends.

Mark smelled the wonderfully sweet fragrance in the air from the flowers again; he really liked that. The candlelight seemed to warm the atmosphere as the twinkling lights gently lit up the dining hall. The ambience was perfect! He couldn't be more pleased with how it all turned out.

Her friends were all seated at the V.I.P table, towards the back of the room especially decorated for the guest of honor. There were ushers escorting late-arriving guests to their designated tables. Lucy knows how to coordinate, that's for sure. Many of Marks co-workers were there to celebrate also, including Nick and his wife Julie. They were very good friends of his, but Julie was especially close to Allie. They were all seated next to Allies' table watching her laugh and carry on.

Allie and her father would make occasional eye contact and make funny faces at each other. Plenty of wonderful food and drinks were being served promptly to the tables, as all the extra staff was very busy. Mark couldn't help but critique the manner in which the new helpers worked, but he reminded himself that tonight was a time to relax and have a good time. Not to micromanage from afar.

Lucy made a short announcement. "Attention everyone... dinner service is almost finished and then after a short while, we will have cake. THEN we will open presents," she concluded with a smile.

Allie smiled warmly at everyone and enjoyed her meal of lamb chops and hearts of palm salad, her favorite.

Mark noticed Julie, who was watching Allie.

"Mark, I still can't believe our little Allie is eighteen already! She looks so grown up in that beautiful dress, too! It's a little frightening," Julie laughed.

"Oh, I know," he agreed. "She joked about the dress on the

way here, she said, "Dad I can't believe for one second, that you picked this out yourself, it doesn't have long sleeves!" I said, "Yeah, but it goes all the way to the floor, doesn't it!" Mark smirked.

Julie laughed out loud and touched his arm.

With a furrowed brow, she poked her head up above the crowd and looked around at the room.

"Is something the matter?" Mark asked, noticing her concern.

"No, I'm just trying to see where Nick has gone off to now. He keeps running off. I think that a certain SOMEBODY needs to tell him he's not working tonight," Julie said sarcastically. "You know, like his boss?"

Mark looked over just in time to see Nick make his way across the room towards their table.

"Here he comes now. I'll remind him," Mark smiled.

"Hey, guys!" Nick looked a little pale, even in the dimly lit room.

"Where did you disappear to?" Julie asked.

"I went to use the bathroom, is that alright?" Nick snapped.

"Are you ok, did you get sick?" Julie asked, noticing his paleness.

"No, I feel fine. Why?" He downed another glass of wine.

"There's no need to worry about anything, Nick. Everything is being taken care of. Relax and just enjoy the evening with your wife," Mark said to him smiling.

Nick laughed nervously. "Yeah, I guess it's just hard to get out of the work mode."

"Try eating some dinner instead of drinking it. Have you had any food yet?" Julie asked.

"Jule's, I'm fine!" Nick said irritated.

Julie playfully waved her hand towards him to dismiss his rotten mood.

Despite his friends bickering, Mark was really enjoying himself. He was mainly watching Allie having all the fun, but he was also having a good time, his self. It had been quite a while since he'd had a night off.

Mark sat back and took in the moment. He thought of his mother in times like this. Mark's mother and sister would be so proud of Allie. He watched as Allie walked over to embrace a friend to thank her for coming. Her smiling face and animated hand gestures made him laugh. Julie chuckled at the same time. Mark realized that she too, was watching Allie again.

"She looks like a graceful little butterfly, fluttering around the room," Julie grinned.

"A social butterfly," he added.

Julie laughed and took a sip of her wine.

"Looks like "Papa Dom" is going to grace us with a toast," Nick said flatly.

Dom was at the head of the room, standing next to Allie, dinging his glass. When the room quieted down he began, "Now I realize this speech of mine is terribly unplanned," he looked in Lucy's direction and pretended to beg for forgiveness. The guests laughed hysterically at this.

"But, I need to say a few things BEFORE we have cake," Dom explained. Everyone was listening now.

"I would like to personally, thank you all for coming to celebrate my god-daughter's eighteenth birthday! It is part of my family's tradition to allow the birthday girl her first sip of wine!" Dom placed a wine glass in front of Allie and held out the bottle of wine.

Mark noticed the bottle was that of the same vintage they had drank earlier, in his office.

As he poured her a glass of wine, the waiters quickly refilled everyone's glasses for the toast. A couple of waitresses were refilling water and soda-pop to those who were not of age. Allie looked at Mark and mouthed the words, "You ok with this?" He nodded and smiled back at her, raising his glass. Dom had asked for Mark's permission earlier that day.

"To friends and family, may you cherish your youth and ensure bright futures. Happy birthday, Princess Allie! You have become a beautiful young woman, and may God continue to bless you in every aspect of your life," Dom's misty eyes betrayed his suddenly gruff tone.

Applause erupted from all around and Allie's friends giggled as they watched her take her first drink of wine. In front of other adults, that is.

"Now, it's time for cake!!" Lucy interrupted.

Mark got up and walked over to stand next to Allie.

The waiters wheeled out the lavishly decorated birthday cake. An acoustic version of "Happy Birthday" began to play in the background. Everyone began to chime in and sing the words. The restaurants staff began to clap in rhythm, and others caught on quickly. The cake glowed with all eighteen candles lit, as Lucy guided Allie towards it to "make her wish."

"Ok, ok, I wish for…" Allie squinted as she silently made her wish…and then blew out all of the candles! (Not in one breathe of course.)

While everyone was being served slices of the beautiful cake, Allie was then presented with her very own, miniature version of the cake. That must have been Lucy's special surprise she had mentioned. Many pictures were being taken as you can imagine, and the flashes of the cameras were beginning to bother Mark's bad eye. Even with the corrective laser surgery, his vision would sometimes blur, which made it hard for him to focus. The old injury was a morbid reminder of how special today was for him. How poignant.

"Happy birthday, Princess, I love you," he said tenderly. She gave him a long hug and said, "Thank you for this dad, I'll never forget this night as long as I live!" Allie turned and exclaimed loudly, "I thank every one of you for a wonderful night, thank you for coming and being a part of the best night of my life!" She cried.

That was Allie, as gracious as she was beautiful.

Mark walked over to the lobby where it was a bit quieter. He stood back and watched as everyone indulged in the delectable cake. He couldn't help but notice the staff was starting to disperse a little. Probably since the food service was officially over. He also had to remind himself, that HE wasn't working tonight either.

Mark looked for Dom, hoping to have caught up with him at some point this evening. Except for the toast, he hadn't seen him much tonight.

Just then, Mark heard a commotion at the head of the room. Mark turned just in time to see Allie slump over into Jen's lap. Everyone was panicking and running to her. He heard someone say, "Call 911!" Dom was suddenly at her side.

"Allie?" Mark yelled. His heart went up into his throat, and it was pounding so hard he could barely talk. Mark was already moving people out of his way, trying to make it through the crowd to get to her. He could see glimpses of Dom laying her on her back. "Move, please! Excuse me!" he yelled.

Too many people were crowding around her, he couldn't get through the hysterical young girls. He jumped onto the table, and slid off the other side, spilling the floating candles. There she was. Dom was already administering C.P.R. and assured him, that "help was on the way." Mark smoothed the hair out of her face and kissed her forehead, "You're going to be ok Allie, you're going to be just fine," he whispered in her ear.

She started to gag and vomit. "Turn her to the side Marko!!" Dom yelled.

Her breathing slowed and became very shallow.

"Allie! Can you hear me? Allie cat, open your eyes, come on honey," Mark tried to shake her to get her to stir. Her skin was clammy, cool and becoming almost translucent.

She started to mumble... "It's ok dad, my wish, my wish came true..."

"What? What was that honey? What did you wish? Tell Daddy! Stay awake," he stammered.

"I wished that Aunt Alice was here with us... and she's right here," Allie smiled faintly as her eyes rolled back into her head.

"Lily!" Mark shouted, not realizing he had said her REAL name. Dom looked at him strangely for a second. "I mean... Allie! Wake up honey! Allie?" Tears fell freely from his eyes. He was suddenly so afraid of losing her.

"Sir, I need you to move, NOW, please! Stand back," Mark

felt a tug on his shoulder.

The E.M.T's were trying to get to her. Mark stood up and backed away... not hearing anything else, but what they were saying. Everyone and everything else seemed muted.

"I can't get a pulse," said the first man.

"Let's bag her, get her in the bus!" The E.M.T.'s were yelling at each other.

"We'll get her hooked up to fluids inside the ambulance," said the second man.

Everything seemed to happen in fast motion after that, Mark ran beside her as they wheeled her out to the ambulance and he grabbed her cool hand for one last squeeze. Why he felt it would be the last, he wasn't sure.

Dom was right by his side, assuring him that everything would be fine. Dom had a car waiting for them to follow the ambulance. Julie was already running to her car as well.

Once at the hospital they were taken to a family waiting room.   Something in the air had changed. Mark insisted that he be at her side, but they gently refused, telling him to please patiently wait for a moment until the Dr. would be able to come in and speak to him. Mark sensed it then. He already knew what they were preparing to tell him.

With Dom, Lucy, and Julie in attendance, Mark was told that Allie was pronounced dead in the ambulance. She had died. She was gone.

They wouldn't know the cause of death until an autopsy was performed. The Doctor thought it could have been an allergic reaction to something she may have eaten or drank. Dom was staring at Mark, watching, waiting for some kind of reaction that never came. Lucy seemed almost afraid of what Mark might do, discouraging any eye contact. No one knew how to react. It was so surreal. Julie began to cry and reached out and grabbed Mark's arm for support. Mark was devoid of any emotion. He just didn't feel anything at all. It was strangely calming and almost peaceful; not to feel anything. It felt like he was dreaming and simply no longer a part of this painful physical world. The Doctor continued to talk, but Mark didn't listen to a word. As long as he didn't believe her death, none of this was real to him.

Dom asked a series of questions to the nurse and proceeded to the desk to speak with the staff. He helped Mark, by making all the necessary arrangements. Mark blindly signed whatever was put in front of him. He didn't care what happened with the paperwork. It wasn't going to change anything.

"Marko, do you want to see her?" Dom asked.

Mark nodded.

"I'll be right there with you," Dom patted his shoulder. "You're not alone, Marko. I'll be right by your side, till you ask me to leave."

A nurse led them to the triage unit where she was laid out. Lucy stayed behind to talk to the others who gathered in the lobby.

Mark could hear his daughters dear friend Jen, sobbing uncontrollably from the waiting area, as she learned the heart breaking news.

The nurse quickly jerked the curtain to the side, with a shrill metal scraping sound.

There she was, his baby girl… his sweet angel. She looked like she was sleeping, so peaceful and dreaming. The three of them stood and looked at her for a moment before Dom and Julie turned and left, quietly closing the curtain behind them. Mark was all alone with her now.

He heard Dom say something to Julie about maybe getting a priest. "I don't need a priest," Mark thought, "I need my daughter to wake up."

Mark looked at Allie's angelic face in disbelief… not truly believing that she was really gone. "She never made a sound when she slept anyway," he thought, as he stood there watching, waiting for her to breathe in deep.

But there was nothing. No sudden gasp or deep breath. Just silence.

Mark was trying to feel something about what was happening. He saw her with his own eyes, yet nothing budged…

He didn't even tear up. He couldn't cry.

It just felt wrong, so unnatural, like it shouldn't be happening. He closed his eyes and took in a few deep breaths. He began to feel something. There was something there, alright, something familiar stirring deep within him. He knew what this was. It was pain; pure sadness, in its truest form to him. That dreaded feeling of emptiness and complete loss that he had felt so long ago.

It started to rise up in him, and he desperately tried to push it back down. He didn't want to hurt again. Instead, he turned it into anger. Anger doesn't hurt as bad, he realized. Maybe he would allow this.

Mark began pacing the small room. He felt compelled to say something to her.

"I made a promise to you a long time ago, baby, that I would protect you and keep you safe and I didn't do that … did I," he was talking out loud to her…. seemingly, apologizing.

He thought of Allie, Alice, and of her baby. What kind of protector was he? Alice and his mother would be so disappointed, wouldn't they? He felt a sharp pain in his chest. It physically hurt him to think that he had let them down in any way.

Suddenly, a large knot seemed to form in his gut. He was on the verge of getting sick. Mark struggled to make sense of the situation.

"Was this a freak accident? Or did someone do this to you, baby?" He whispered to her as he knelt down next to her head.

This is really happening, isn't it, he asked himself. His mind was reeling.

"You really are lying here, and you're never going to get up, are you?" he said out loud.

He felt the sting of the tears coming now, as he looked at his sleeping angel; so pretty, like a porcelain doll. Mark gently stroked her hair back off her face, careful not to touch her skin. He didn't want to feel the coldness in her normally flushed cheeks that were usually so full of life. He steadied himself against the stretcher and fought the impending urge to vomit. He struggled with the reasoning aspect of it. Despite his need to understand, he would never accept the loss of his precious daughter.

Mark wiped away a tear on the sleeve of his shirt. He thought about what the Doctor had said, "it could have been a possible food allergy". He remembered Allie throwing up. It was a plausible explanation, but that still didn't sit well. He hadn't known her to be allergic to anything, and they definitely wouldn't have served it at her party if she were. It felt wrong. A random thought quickly entered his mind. "This might not have been an accident. It could be a poisoning," he thought. Was it morbid for him to think that? The old "Detective" mind set began to focus his thoughts on a possible homicide case. He needed a motive.

Why would anyone want to do this to her? What could the motive possibly be, and how could it involve Allie? He just felt like this wasn't an accident. His intuition had beckoned him again. Who did he know, that was capable of killing a precious young woman? Allie had no enemies. She was just a young girl with her whole life ahead of her, a completely innocent.... young woman.

Just then, his body physically answered his own questions.

The hair on his arms and legs, spiked at the sudden realization. His mind quickly revealed the possibility.

This was an unmistakable moment of clarity for Mark.

There was only one person he knew of that was truly capable of such horror. This particular person also had something against him and he wouldn't hesitate to kill another innocent young woman, especially, if it were in the name of revenge.

"No!" Mark said aloud. "No, it couldn't be."

How could he have found us? Mark thought. He's still in prison! Marks mind was spiraling out of control just trying to rationalize this insane notion. That doesn't make any sense… Mark struggled with his sudden awareness. His parole hearing is coming up… would he jeopardize his freedom for a little revenge?

The sudden, knowledgeable fear he felt slowly began to manifest itself into something else. It was strange, but familiar. It slowly filled his heart and soul with every breath he took.

Mark felt the anger turn to silent rage as it consumed his entire being. He could feel it wrapping around his heart, like the welcoming arms of an old friend's embrace.

He stood over Allie, kissing her on the top of her head for the last time.

Mark said his name out loud…"Leo Vanzetti," he hissed.

"Did you have something to do with this?" he whispered

quietly and looked up to the ceiling.

Mark's instincts forced him to acknowledge the possible connection. His mind instantly reacted, and gave him his answer. In Mark's heart and mind, this was the only possible explanation. He had his first suspect.

"He has managed to take everything from me now," Mark's voice was low and raw.

He looked down at Allie, making a final promise to her. Mark vowed, "He's taken everything good in my life, now. I won't stop, until I have taken HIS."

CHAPTER 3

SHIFT CHANGE

Dom was standing at the nurse's station when Mark came out of the viewing room from seeing Allie.

"Marko," Dom nodded respectfully, acknowledging him.

"I am handling all of the preparations here at the hospital including the autopsy scheduling. There's no need for you to worry about funeral arrangements right now," Dom stated. He was very concerned for Mark. He was genuinely trying to ease some of his worry.

"Thank you, but I can take care of all that myself," Mark arched his back, stretching his strained neck. All though, he wasn't ready to deal with or even hear of "arrangements" just yet. It was nice of Dom.

"Nonsense, it's already done. Would you like to stay awhile or shall I take you to a priest? Whatever you need, just ask," Dom said. He pinched the bridge of his nose, and rubbed his eyes. He looked very tired as well.

Mark felt a fleeting hint of relief. He was grateful to Dom for handling the specifics, but he really could've handled it.

"Alright, thank you, my friend," Mark put his pride aside. He was too exhausted to argue.

"Why don't you get Lucy home and I will call you if I hear anything. I need to go say a few words to her friends and their worried parents. Then I think I'll head back to the house," Mark said.

Dom gave Mark a puzzled look.

"You could come to our home. If you prefer not to be alone, I will wait here for you," Dom urged.

"I'll be fine, I really don't want to be around people right now. I need to be alone tonight." Mark thought for a moment about what that actually meant to him... to be alone. Without Allie, he had nothing. Nothing would ever be worthwhile. LIFE would have no real meaning any longer. He really was, all alone.

Dom studied Marks face and reactions, wondering what he was thinking about.

"Alright, Marko I understand," Dom said reluctantly. Marks tone of voice then changed. It sounded unusually chipper, as he said, " Have a good night! I'll be in contact."

Dom paused. "I still need to discuss my week's plans with

you. I hope that you'll understand my predicament," Dom seemed hesitant. "I must leave tomorrow, to tend to my sister Anita's health care issues and I don't want you to think that I'm insensitive to this situation."

Mark raised his hand to quiet him, knowing where the conversation was going.

"Please, don't worry about this. Okay? Go. Take care of your sister, and I will let you know what's going on as soon as I find out anything." Dom looked very upset and quite emotional. In fact, Mark had never seen him this way in the eleven years they'd known each other. On the other hand, they've never experienced this kind of tragedy... together.

Mark tried to reassure him.

"I don't know what's going to happen, or when it might... so please, just do what you have to do. Focus on your family and do what's right by them. That's how you can help me," Mark said honestly.

Mark sincerely meant every word and Dom knew that. He nodded quickly and cleared his throat, patting Mark hard on the shoulder. That sentiment meant more to Dom that Mark would ever know.

"Okay, Marko. Lucy will handle the restaurant with Nick, and my niece will be here tomorrow. She'll be hosting this week and filling in where needed. I will return as soon as I find Anita a new home health care nurse and everything is to my liking. I will definitely be back on Monday, as I have made it clear that the autopsy be scheduled no sooner than that day. I will be around to handle things at that time," Dom finished.

They stopped just before rounding the corner, and entering the waiting room. Something about that didn't sit well with Mark.

"YOU made it clear that the autopsy be scheduled later? Isn't that something that the coroner usually dictates?" Mark didn't realize he was glaring at Dom. "What if they were able to perform it sooner?" he asked.

"Yes, well, I felt that it was appropriate timing, what with the holiday on Monday and all. No reason other than wanting answers and personally seeing to the scheduling. It's important to make sure these things go smoothly, yes?" Dom stared strangely at Mark for an awkward moment. "It was the soonest for the hospital staff anyhow. I'm only trying to help you."

Mark realized that he might have sounded a little rude. His pride reared its head… once again. He took a slow deep breath to calm himself. Perhaps he was overthinking the issue.

"You're right, who knows how long it could be before they are able to do it, anyway. That's very helpful, thank you. Thanks for all you've done, it won't be forgotten."

"You're welcome." Dom smiled.

Dom handed Mark some wrapped up tissues, and Mark put them in his jacket pocket. "Just in case you need them, there's no shame in it." Dom squeezed Marks shoulder. "This too, shall pass."

They walked into the waiting room to a sea of sobbing faces. Dom and Lucy left almost immediately.

Mark went to Jen first and held her for a moment and spoke a few words of thanks to her parents. He told them about the autopsy coming up after the long weekend and to expect a funeral service the following weekend. Jen mentioned wanting to have a candle light vigil the following Tuesday, when school resumed, and he thanked her for her thoughtfulness. He knew Allie would've appreciated that.

Mark felt emotionally detached, which felt a bit inappropriate to him. He was eerily calm. He felt phony and awkward talking to these worried and absolutely distraught people. He went through each conversation like he was reciting a rehearsed speech, person after person.

"Thank you so much for your kind words, Allie would appreciate that. I'll let everyone know as soon as I learn of anything new. I'm very grateful, that she had you in her life. Thank you again for your condolences." That was basically the speech in a nut shell.

It was after midnight by the time everyone dispersed; all except for one.

She sat huddled in the corner, looking out the window. Her legs were curled up to her chest, covered by her jacket. She turned her head to look at him as she wiped her reddened puffy eyes with a stiff napkin she'd gotten from the lobby's coffee station.

"Aw, shit, Jule's? I didn't see you there, I'm sorry. I would have come over sooner to speak with you as well," Mark quickly walked over to her, offering her his hand as she sluggishly tried to stand.

"I already know what you're going to say, Mark, there's no need for you to recite it all for me," she smiled a half smile and stood to greet him. She got to her feet and looked into his eyes. Not caring what it may look like to anyone else, she wrapped her arms around him and hugged him.

Mark felt compassion for her... and was reminded of how he oddly felt nothing for himself. He wondered if he were in shock, and thought that the normal grieving feelings would come soon enough.

"And Nick, is he here too?" Mark stepped away from Julie and pretended to look around. Mark hadn't seen Nick since the party, back at Angelo's Restaurant.

"No, he's not here. He took my car home to get some sleep. He drove your car here though, so you'd have it. He has an early morning but, wanted to give you his deepest condolences," she shook her head and her brow crinkled, like she was annoyed by what she had just said.

"Oh, I understand. That was... very thoughtful of him to bring my car. What about you, though? Do you need a ride home then?" Mark asked.

What a peculiar thing to do, Mark thought. It was nice of his friend to bring his car, but to leave his wife without? Mark was tired and was probably over thinking things again... so he let it go.

"I had planned on taking a cab, but I would like that very much, thank you," Julie stared at Mark like she was sizing up a stranger. "Are you ok to drive, Mark?" Her voice came out sounding weak and shaky. "Maybe we should split a cab."

"I'm okay, Julie, as good as could be expected, you know? I can drive. I promise I won't kill us," he tried to joke around, but the joke fell flat. Once again, he realized how inappropriate he seemed to be acting.

Mark noticed the sudden tears welling up in Julie's eyes.

"Hey, don't cry. That wasn't funny, I'm sorry. Don't worry about me, though, it must be adrenaline or something. I'm not going to wreck us, I promise," he said reassuringly.

He absentmindedly put his arms around her. For a brief second, he put his hand on the back of her head, feeling her soft blonde hair, and tenderly held her to him. Then he abruptly let her go.

She stopped crying, and cleared her throat.

"I have confidence in your driving abilities. I'm pretty tired and I just don't know what to say except, I'm sorry. My brain isn't functioning, I'm so sorry," Julie rambled.

She was weeping as she fumbled with her jacket, and mumbling something about her hands not doing what she wanted them to do. She struggled to pull her coat up over her shoulders. Mark saw this, and helped her.

He realized that she was taking this pretty hard, much worse than he appeared to be handling it. He knew that she had loved Allie like her own daughter. They had grown very close over the years.

"You don't have to keep apologizing, Jules, really. I know you're exhausted. Let's just get you home, huh?" He tried his best to reassure her, and gave her the best smile he could muster.

Julie suddenly burst into tears, as she cried out...

"I saw her! I snuck in after you and talked to her. I had to say goodbye and I think I had to make sure she was really gone!" She was choking on her words. Julie covered her eyes with her hands, like she could block him from seeing what she had seen...

"Shhh... it's okay," he whispered quietly to her. "That's just fine, it's more than fine, and I understand why you did that. I did it too." He pulled out the wad of extra tissues from his pocket, offering them to her. Hugging her close to his side, he slowly proceeded towards the elevator doors. They walked by the nurse's station for the last time. Mark looked up to thank them, but instead saw new, curious faces. Must have been a shift change, he thought. So with a respectful goodnight nod, they walked on by.

CHAPTER 4

THE CALL OF DUTY

"Oh, no," Julie mumbled. She sat up in the passenger seat. She had closed her eyes and drifted off for a moment.

"What is it? What's the matter?" Mark turned his head slightly, not taking his eyes off the road.

"I needed to go back to the restaurant, but never mind that, I'll go there first thing in the morning. There's no reason for you to go back there. Everyone's pro-probably gone anyway," she stammered.

"No, it's fine actually. I'll take you. Did you leave something behind?" Mark asked curiously.

"Yes, my cell phone. I must have left it there on the table in all of the…um…commotion. Like I said, I'll just get it in the morning," she nodded convincingly and tried to smile, "Or, I could ask Nick to grab it for me," Julie mentioned.

"It's not a problem Julie. I'm sure the police are still there, It's only been a few hours. I was headed there anyway." He was thinking about the crime scene, and wanted to see it. He might still be able to talk to the investigators. Mark was more than willing to take her there, he was eager.

Julie nodded and replied, "Okay, thank you." All though, she couldn't imagine why he'd want to go back there.

As they pulled into the parking lot, Mark realized that almost everyone HAD left. A couple police cars remained; one of them was unmarked. "Probably, a homicide detective," Mark thought.

There was also a service van of some kind and Julie's car. They parked around back to go in through the service doors. Mark took out his personal work keys and tried the door, but it was already unlocked. He quickly entered, expecting the alarm to start beeping, but it didn't.

This was unusual, and it annoyed Mark. The back door was supposed to be locked at all times. Maybe, Mark thought, the alarm had been shut off to accommodate the police detectives. He guessed it made sense that they be able to come and go as needed. Mark quickly rationalized this, and let it go. He realized how paranoid he had become, and should probably cut himself some slack.

Mark slowly lead Julie inside, and looked around. An unfamiliar looking janitor looked up at them, as he mopped the floor. Mark and Julie carefully made their way through the slippery kitchen and went out into the main dining hall. There were a couple of temp-workers vacuuming and taking down the lights as well.

Mark glanced over to what was once "Allie's table" and saw nothing but a tidy place setting. He couldn't smell the flowers anymore; not even a trace of them. It was almost as if they had never been there; never existed.

"Mark? Julie? What in the hell, are you guys doing here?" The sound of Nick's voice brought him back to reality. Nick was shocked to see Mark standing there. He looked like he had just seen a ghost.

Nick had just come out of Dom's office and was walking down the hallway with a much taller man.

"Mark, um… this is the cop that's doing the investigation, he just had some questions, and so, I handled it," Nick straightened his back, proud of his contribution.

"Thank you, Nick. Also, thank you for bringing my car to the hospital earlier, I appreciate that very much," Mark said.

"Oh, yeah, you're welcome. It was nothing," Nick smiled. "Anything I can do to help, man."

"I think I might have left my phone on the table," Julie said from behind Mark.

"Oh, yeah, I put that in the office," Nick said. He was still staring at Mark. "Go ahead and grab it."

"Mark… Anderson?" The investigator asked.

"Yes, sir, I'm the father of the young girl who died here this evening," Mark answered nonchalantly.

The background noises and the whirring of the vacuum had stopped.

The two workers had apparently been eavesdropping on their conversation, as they were now staring at Mark with large, frightened eyes.

"Yes, sir, I'm aware of that, and I'm very sorry for your loss," the man said kindly.

"My name is Detective Williams," he introduced himself and extended his hand. Detective Williams was a tall man, a couple of inches taller than Mark, actually, maybe 6'3". His most notable attribute, however, was his firm handshake.

"It's nice to meet you, Detective Williams. Thank you for your kind words," Mark glanced at the woman who had been vacuuming, as she quickly turned it back on and looked to the ground.

"I'm curious to know where the investigation lies at this point. If you don't mind taking a walk with me, I would like to hear about it and learn of how everything has developed so far," Mark turned his back towards Nick and escorted Williams to the dining room.

Julie was encouraging Nick to start making their way

towards the office to retrieve her phone. She was saying something about wanting to get home, while Nick ignored her, still trying to listen to Mark and the Detectives conversation.

"The crime scene team has been here already and has taken pictures, collected certain evidence and I've been interviewing witnesses. I was just finishing up with Mr. Butler actually," Detective Williams added.

Mark glanced back at the two women vacuuming, to make sure that they had, indeed, gone back to work.

"What kinds of "certain evidence?" Mark inquired.

Detective Williams continued to walk along side Mark as he explained.

"There were a few perishable items that needed to be tested, and some finger printing, but that is a standard in any case," he said, modestly.

Mark came to a stop in front of the main table and folded his arms. "I understand," Mark scratched the back of his head. "Please excuse my sudden impatient nature; I'm usually not like this," he lowered his voice as he spoke directly to the Detective.

"But, between you and me, I'm familiar with the standard procedures of an investigation. If you don't mind, I would like you to be frank with me and explain it as if you were speaking to a fellow officer. I hope you understand," Mark stated.

Detective Williams looked at Mark for a moment; his blue

eyes squinting. He understood completely.

"Alright then, Mr. Anderson, I do," Detective Williams cleared his throat.

"The certain "perishable items" that I mentioned, were slices of cake taken from each of the cakes, the victims, and the main birthday cake intended for the guests. We felt it needed to be examined and tested immediately. Also, wine glasses, cups and silverware were printed, and most of the waiters and waitresses were interviewed. Many dispersed quickly after the incident, but we were able to attain thirteen eye witness accounts. Some of these statements were from wait staff, some were guests. Perhaps, we could get a list of ALL of the people that were working here tonight, just in case we need to further question anyone, all though it may not be necessary..." Detective Williams chose his next words carefully.

"However, things seem pretty straight forward at this point," he averted Mark's eye contact.

"I'll have Nick get you a complete list of the staff's names in the morning. I would also kindly ask, for you to call me, personally, whenever you are privy to any new information," Mark asked. Detective Williams nodded in approval.

"My daughter's autopsy won't be conducted until sometime after Monday, so I won't have their findings or a definitive cause of death at least, until then. But, I would appreciate any information that you have beforehand. Also, with all due respect, Detective, this case is anything but straight forward," they began to walk again reaching the main dining hall.

"Absolutely, Mr. Anderson; I meant no disrespect. I'll call you if there are any changes," Detective Williams hesitated, "I don't mean to be insensitive, but might I ask you a few questions? I mean, tomorrow, obviously would be a better time. It's just that with the nature of the events, it's best to get the freshest recollection possible from a witness. I can imagine you would like to get some rest though," Detective Williams glanced at his watch. It was damn near one o'clock in the morning.

"No, I don't mind at all. Now, is just as good a time as any, please... have a seat," Mark said collectedly. He gestured towards an empty chair.

"I appreciate your willingness to accommodate my requests. If there's anything I can do to help you, then I have all the time in the world," Mark said truthfully.

Mark heard Nick jingling his keys as he and Julie entered the main dining hall; they were heading home. Julie walked up to them and handed both Mark and Detective Williams, a bottle of water.

"Thank you, Ma'am," Detective Williams said.

Mark smiled and nodded at her kind gesture. "Thanks, Jules," he glanced at Nick.

"And thank you, for answering the Detectives questions and helping out extra at the restaurant this next week. I appreciate it. You should go home and get some rest now," Mark said sincerely. Nick hugged him quickly... and awkwardly.

Nick assured Mark he would be there in the morning, and would "definitely" provide Mr. Williams with a complete list of the wait staff from the temp agency. Nick walked out, with an exhausted Julie in tow. Mark thanked them again for all their kindness and said good night as he locked the door behind them. Mark returned to the table, and for the first time all night, he sat down.

Mark politely and honestly answered a series of random questions leading up to the tragic event itself. Detective Williams was very respectful in his questioning.

Mark had just gotten up again to let out the last of the cleaning crew, when he came back to the table and stood for a moment, deep in thought.

"You seem like a thorough detective, Mr. Williams," Mark said, respectively.

"Thank you, Mr. Anderson. I like to think so," he smiled and took a drink of his water.

"Please, call me Mark," he said as he took his seat across from Detective Williams.

"I would like to ask YOU a few questions now if that's alright," asked Mark.

"Oh, of course," Detective Williams straightened up in his chair. "Any questions you have, just feel free to ask. I'll answer whatever I can, Mark."

Mark had already anticipated this. He thought the Detective to be very forthcoming.

"Do you have a family of your own, Detective?" Mark asked bluntly.

Detective Williams was surprised by the sudden personal question. He had just assumed the questioning would be regarding the investigation.

"I …am divorced. I have a daughter, but she lives with her mother," he said honestly.

"Aw... a tell-tale sign of a devoted Detective," Mark smirked.

"I suppose so," Williams stared at him intently. "What does this have to do with the investigation?" Detective Williams asked.

"Do you get to see her much? Your daughter, that is," Mark continued.

"No. Well, I used to get her every other weekend until her mother moved to Washington State about a year ago. She doesn't come down that often anymore," Detective Williams looked uncomfortable.

"That's a shame, I'm sorry to hear it," he said sadly. "How long have you been a Detective?" Mark asked curiously.

Detective Williams took a deep breath. "Well, I was a police officer for eleven years, and I've been a homicide detective now, for almost five-" Williams paused.

"And how about you, how long were YOU an officer, Mr. Anderson?" He asked cautiously, reversing the questioning back to Mark.

Mark smiled wide and laughed out loud. Mark was entertained by Williams' impressive observation.

Detective Williams smiled as he waited for his answer.

"It seems like it was a very long time ago," Mark said calmly.

He was suddenly aware of how dry and parched his mouth and throat had become. Mark opened his bottle of water and drank most of it down in three, large gulps.

Mark absentmindedly rubbed the back of his neck as he remembered. He put down the bottle carefully, and began to answer the question. "I joined the Army in '90 and served during Operation Desert Storm. I took some metal shrapnel in my neck, and lower back, courtesy of a tank explosion. Somehow, all my major arteries and organs were spared and I was sent home a few months later with an honorable discharge. My mother was so thankful that I wouldn't be going back. I secretly felt like I was being benched on the side lines of a championship game. So, I decided I wanted to "serve and protect". I was a regular beat cop, patrol, and an aspiring narcotics agent right out of the academy and I had a great partner. I called him Sarge. I did well, despite being so young. They said I had a knack for reading people, and had sharp survival instincts," Mark looked intently at Detective

Williams.

Detective Williams listened carefully, intrigued by his story.

"My father was never around. He and my mother divorced when I was eight. I saw him maybe once after that. It was just me, my mother, and my little sister Alice. She was only three years old when he left. I did the best I could to help take care of us. I stayed in school and when I turned twelve, I worked any job I could get to help put food on the table. I thought if I joined the Army, I would get my college paid for, and get out of Jersey. That only lasted a year. My mother had found out that she had breast cancer and didn't tell me about it until after I had gotten home from the war. She died nine months later, just after I graduated from the Academy."

"I sort of, lost my moral compass and drowned my sorrows quite frequently. I met a woman at a bar and had a few one night stands with her and she became pregnant. We weren't together or dating; nothing quite like that, so she decided to have an abortion. She just wanted to move on with her life, but by the time she got in there, the Dr. said she was too far along. I don't believe in abortion, and I tried to reason with her. I was relieved when I heard the Doctors news. Her new plan was to give the baby up for adoption. She said it was her choice and I had nothing to do with it. So, my sister Alice and I convinced her that she could hand the baby over to us and walk away, no questions asked. She did just that. I decided that I loved that baby regardless of whether I was the real father or not. I wasn't going to be like my father, and take off," Mark paused.

"The state had a paternity test done, and she was, in fact, mine. Alice laughed and said, "as if there were any doubt! She's a mini you!" Mark chuckled at the memory.

He started to feel his nose tingle, like accidently breathing in water in a swimming pool. Mark put his emotion in check and became serious again.

"I'm about to ask you something very important, Detective. I can sense that you're honest and hardworking. But what I'm wondering about you, is a bit more personal. How far would you go in order to bring justice to an innocent girl?" Mark asked seriously. "Would you go beyond the normal call of duty?"

Detective Williams was caught off guard, and looked directly at this curious man across from him.

"Of course I would, Mark. Do you suspect foul play?" He asked, fascinated.

"I SUSPECT a lot of things, but I'll tell you what I KNOW. I know that things are never usually what they seem. I know that what happened to my daughter was no accident. I also know whose behind it, and I don't want them to get away with it," Mark looked very calm, and confident.

The Detectives mind was trying to process this sudden revelation. Should he just keep this odd theory in the back of his mind and humor Mark? Maybe just keep a close eye on him, weighing more on the side of caution. Mark didn't seem crazy. What if, this guy is telling the truth? He obviously believes it. What if, there was more to this case, than what there appeared to be, and if he was right, then this is a serious case. What if, it was his own daughter?" Williams thought quickly.

"Are you willing to help me investigate my daughter's possible murder?" Mark asked frankly.

Mark's vulnerability shone through in that fleeting moment. But even just for that brief second, Williams saw it, and knew it was the real deal. He made his decision. This man needed his help, and his gut feeling told him it was the right thing to do.

"Yes, I am. I'm willing to help you," Williams stated.

"Wonderful, I thank you. I also appreciate you taking the time to talk to me. Would you be able to come to my home tomorrow to discuss this further?" Mark asked.

"Absolutely, is there a time that's more convenient than others?" Detective Williams was exhausted and ready to call it a night, or a day actually. It was nearly 2:00 a.m.

"No, anytime is good, let me give you my card," Mark sensed that the Detective was ready to go.

Mark wrote down his address on the back of a restaurant business card and gave it to Detective Williams. They stood and began walking towards the doors. "I'll call you first thing in the morning Detective," Mark said.

"Formalities aside, my friends call me Williams," he extended his hand to Mark.

"During and after my football years, everyone called me Williams like it was my first name. I'm sure a solid young man like you played a little ball in high school, you understand!" He joked lightly as Mark walked him out.

"You would have thought my name was Williams, Williams," he continued.

"Well, we have something in common then, Williams," Mark held the door open and Williams stepped out.

"My friends call me Mark, and that isn't my real name either," he smiled.

CHAPTER 5

ONCE UPON A TIME

Williams showed up at Mark's house the following morning at 9:00 a.m. sharp. They sat across from each other at the kitchen table, sipping coffee, as Mark began his story. Williams patiently waited and anticipated what this man needed to tell him. He was intrigued, to say the least.

"My real name is Vincenzo Santoro Lentini. Along with my daughter Lily, I have been in a witness relocation program for the last thirteen years. I testified in a murder trial that convicted Leonardo Vanzetti of two counts of first degree murder. I essentially helped put away my sister and his own brother's killer."

"Leo was a known trouble maker, and was involved in a mess of illegal activity. He was also connected to drug trafficking and local arms dealers. Leo's parents went bankrupt paying for his defense lawyers. They had tried to say that he was mentally incompetent to stand trial for the murders, but his psych evaluation proved otherwise. The Defense had conjured up all these crazy notions that supposedly explained how his actions were the direct influence of the DRUGS and not the conscious decision of the MAN that committed the murders. They presented an interesting argument that if they rehabilitated the man from drugs, then it would eliminate the threat, and he would no longer be a menace to society. They put up a good fight, even if it was a losing battle. He was convicted of two counts of first degree murder."

"But, on the day of sentencing, however, the Judge obviously sympathized with Leo's parents. They told stories of emotional and financial difficulty. They lost not only their youngest son, their family restaurant and now their oldest son to the prison system. Shortly after the trial was over, Mr. Vanzetti, Leo's father, suffered a fatal heart attack," Mark respectively lowered his head.

"Leo was given life WITH the possibility of parole, serving no less than twelve years. He would receive treatment for his drug addiction and his anger issues there. He was to be a candidate for a new rehabilitation program in the state of New Jersey," Mark explained sarcastically.

"Lily and I moved here and assumed the identities of Mark and Allison Anderson. My daughter was barely five when we moved, and obviously knew her name, so I called her Allie, because it sounded similar to Lily."

A sudden memory of a bright eyed, five year old Lily flashed into his head.

Refusing to succumb to his mental distraction, he continued. "I was given a job at Angelo's restaurant as a dish washer, set up by the protection agency. Dom Angelo, being the generous man he is, quickly promoted me to waiting tables. Whenever there was an opportunity for a raise, he thought of me. So, I became the bartender for a while and then before I knew it, I was a shift supervisor, and about two years ago, he made me Restaurant Manager. Nick was the first friend I made here. He was bussing tables when I started, now he's a shift supervisor in training."

"We've been good friends thru it all. His wife, Julie, works in the neonatal intensive care unit at St. Luke's. They don't have any children, and are quite close to us as well. Julie was always involved with Allie. Julie is more of a motherly figure to her, than a friend, or was anyway.   Dom met Lucy a few years ago and they were just married last spring. They don't have any children from previous marriages and they loved Lily as well. We're pretty much all like one big happy family here," Mark concluded.

Mark explained the daily routines they all had, and anything else that he could think of that might be helpful.

Williams sat and sipped his coffee, listening to everything Mark had to say. He occasionally wrote something down on his crisp and scratchy notepad. Williams adjusted his glasses and nodded his head diligently.

"Have you been in contact with your witness protection coordinator?" He asked.

"Yes. I called first thing this morning. Vanzetti is still in prison... for now anyway. He coincidentally, has a parole hearing on Monday morning. However, my coordinator has assured me that he is "well aware of the events that have transpired and feels this has been a terrible tragedy, a mere accident," Mark said mockingly.

"You have got to be shitting me. He has a parole hearing... this Monday?" Williams was shocked. He definitely understood why Mark was so skeptical now.

"They seem to think that this has NOTHING to do with Vanzetti, at all. This is why I need you to help me all the more. This is going to be a tough pill for some people to swallow," Mark continued to plead his case to Williams.

"What I would like you to do is quite reasonable. I have no unrealistic expectations from you, Williams. I simply need a fresh pair of eyes and ears, looking for facts and clues to help piece together this puzzle. I need solid evidence to prove his connection. You and I both know that I can't go to the police and expose my identity with nothing but conjecture and theory," Mark said sincerely.

"I do understand that," Williams hesitated. "Alright, let me make sure I got this straight. I'm just going to think out loud for a moment, if that's all right. "Williams took off his glasses and rubbed the sore indentation on the bridge of his nose. "May I speak frankly?"

"Of course," Mark waited politely.

Williams concentrated on every word, trying to make sense

of it all as he spoke. "You think, or feel strongly anyway, that Leo Vanzetti, or quite possibly someone connected to him, somehow discovered your new identity and found your location. He then had your daughter murdered and made it look like some sort of an accident. All of this being his retaliation, for your testimony against him at your sister's murder trial, which in turn, put him away these past thirteen years?" Williams asked. "That's quite the reach," Williams just wanted to state the obvious.

Mark looked at him steadily. "Yes, that's exactly what I think. I believe it indefinitely, with every molecule in my brain. That man is a cold blooded killer. He has never once admitted guilt for the murders, ever. God only knows what has gone on in his mind, being locked up all this time. His resentment towards me, I'm sure, has been unbearable. There's NO doubt in my mind that he's been waiting and planning to take some sort of revenge. He's too proud and stubborn of a man to have just let this all go. The motive is clear to me," Mark said eloquently.

"Alright then, now we just have to prove it," Williams agreed.

Williams then slid his glasses back on.

"First things first, let's go over the preliminary report from the hospital that Dom gave you. It states… possible food contamination or Allergic Reaction. The official cause of death might not be determined for weeks and the autopsy won't be performed until next week you said?" William asked.

"Yeah, that's right," Mark said.

"So for now, we go with the E.M.T's cause of death, which is "anaphylactic shock and asphyxiation," he looked focused as he read the report that Mark put in front of him. "This could coincide with either theory of an allergic reaction or a poisoning," Williams seemed disappointed by this.

Mark had already realized this. "Absolutely, it's disheartening, but we must find other proof that supports that this case is a homicide."

It wasn't easy hearing how she may have died or that she might have suffered. He suddenly thought of her laid out on that cold, metal viewing table.

Mark quickly put the image out of his mind. He continued.

"It's important that we maintain trust between us. I have told you all this because…... I simply don't know who I can trust anymore. I need your help. It's imperative that you know everything, EVERY little thing. I know that he found us, and had someone carry out my daughters murder as a message that he's coming after me…..there's no need to keep up false pretenses."

"He's almost out on parole, and he'll be coming for me. I'll be ready for him… but, let's just do what we can now, in the time that we have, to prove her death wasn't an accident. It was a deliberate, calculated and pre-meditated act. I just know it." Mark didn't realize how loud his voice had become or how agitated it sounded.

"Mark, I know if something ever happened to my daughter, I would do whatever it took to find out the truth. I will help you as much as I'm possibly capable of. I would like to give you my anonymity on this, I really would, but if it turns dangerous then I will need to notify my Captain and bring him in on it," Williams said quietly.

Mark leaned forward and placed his hands in front of him on the table. He looked up into Williams face.

"I understand your position. I also appreciate your forth right attitude, and I respect your personal duty to your job. However, when this turns dangerous… and it will, I will no longer be needing your services," Mark leaned back in his chair.

Williams was perplexed by this.

"I'm sorry. I don't understand.   I'm a detective, Mark. Would you really expect me to just turn my back, if something truly criminal is happening?" Williams seemed bothered and maybe a little perplexed by Marks odd requirement.

Mark folded his hands in his lap, and appeared calm once again. "Something truly criminal has ALREADY happened. Look, it's very important to me that you understand something. I'm not interested in any harm coming to you or any other innocent person around me. I'm not asking you to turn a blind eye to anything. I will do whatever it is that I have to do. I simply need a second pair of eyes, ears and the use of your contacts. You are free to walk away at any time, including now. Once I have the proof that I need, to show that Vanzetti IS involved, I will let you handle it as you see fit and take it to the proper authorities. My daughter's death will not be in vain. You have my word on that," Mark said honestly.

Williams sat back and thought about this proposal. He understood the demands perfectly well, and knew what Mark was asking of him. He also knew that Mark would go forward with this investigation, with or without him. All though Mark didn't show it, Williams knew he was desperate for his help.

Detective Williams leaned forward and extended his hand. He understood that this man needed his help, and if there was anything that he could do to bring him peace and his daughter some justice, he would do it. Mark shook his hand and the deal was silently sealed.

"Let's see who's been visiting Mr. Vanzetti in prison, shall we?" Williams picked up his cell phone and took a deep breath.

CHAPTER 6

COFFEE CUPS

Mark had fallen asleep in Allie's room where he had spent most of the afternoon. He had wandered in and looked around, hoping to feel somewhat close to her. He had only meant to sit down on her bed for a moment, when he reached out and grabbed her pillow. Bunching it up in his hands, he buried his face into the squishy material. Mark inhaled deeply as the lilac scent of Allie's shampoo comforted him.

Waking up instantly out of a sound sleep had startled him. Mark's heart beat quickly as the dull throbbing of it pulsated into his ears. He sat up quickly feeling a sudden poke and scrape on the back of his neck, his hand instantly searching the stinging area. He turned his head and looked down at a feather poking out from her down pillow. He pulled it out, snapping it in his fingers. Mark silently took it as a sign that he just wasn't allowed to sleep peacefully; ever. He heard several quiet knocks at the back door. That sound is probably what woke him up in the first place.

He stood quickly and drew his handgun from the back of his jeans and went downstairs. He held it down low, pointing it away from him, and towards the ground. Mark wouldn't go anywhere now, without his gun or his twin pistols strapped under his jacket. Slowly approaching the back door, he could see the silhouette of a woman through the sheer curtain. It was Julie. He slipped the handgun behind his back and tucked it into his belt, and unlocked the door.

"Hey, come in. Sorry to keep you waiting. Have you been out here long?" He asked, looking around the drive way.

"Not at all… I left work a little early and wanted to check in on you and see how you were holding up," she walked past him as he held the door open for her. He smelled her perfume. Or maybe it was her hair. He couldn't ever get close enough to tell.

Julie dropped her purse on the table, with a thud, and sat down. That's where Allie would've sat, Mark thought to himself.

He noticed Julie's puffy eyes and dark circles. She'd obviously had a rough day as well. He locked the back door and walked around the counter into the kitchen. He took the coffee container out of the fridge, and walked over to the coffee pot.

"Would you like some coffee?" Mark asked. "I was just about to make some."

"Sure, I would love some thank you," Julie managed a smile.

Julie watched him move about in the kitchen. She tried not to stare, but was all too aware that he wasn't wearing a shirt. Too polite to bring it up and ask about them, she'd also noticed the many scars on his chest and back. She also hadn't realized he was so…. muscular. She followed the scar from between his wide shoulder blades down to the middle of his back. Her eyes averted a little lower…

He pulled out two white coffee cups and sat them on the sparkling black granite counter top.

"So you got some sleep today then, huh? That's good," she said awkwardly. Julie smiled and gestured to his unruly hair.

He ran his fingers through his hair, trying to smooth it out. "Yeah, I didn't mean to, but I accidentally fell asleep."

"Well, as long as it was an accident. You're forgiven," she joked.

Mark reached into his pocket and checked his phone for any text messages from Williams as he sat down at the bar. There were none.

"I've got some things to do, that's all. I don't have time to sleep," he snapped his phone shut. "Is Nick still at the restaurant?" Mark wondered why he hadn't heard from his friend yet.

"Probably, he said he would be home for a little bit to have dinner, before heading back to close up. Why don't you join us?

Something tells me you haven't eaten," Julie looked at him, concerned. She tried extra hard to focus and to look him in his eyes, but it was just too tempting to look down at his chest... and his waist. Good lord, his abs were practically begging her to wrap her legs around them. She quickly looked away and shook off the fantasy.

Mark noticed Julie was looking at him. He then realized that he was possibly making Julie uncomfortable by not wearing a shirt. He hadn't exposed his scars to anyone before, not even Allie. Mark was careful to always remain covered for this very reason.

"I'll be right back." Mark went up to his room and quickly pulled on a shirt. He didn't care if it was clean or not. He sat on the bed for a second, pondering Julies invite.

Julie sat quietly, awkwardly looking around the kitchen. She knew that he had probably gone off to put on a shirt. "Way to go, Jule's. Way to stare at the poor man and make him self-conscience," she scolded herself.

Suddenly, a sputtering sound indicating that the pot was almost ready, reminded Mark of the coffee. He quickly walked down the stairs and sauntered over to fill their mugs, handing one over to Julie at the table and taking a seat for himself, at the breakfast bar.

"Thank you for the dinner offer, but, I've got some things to take care of," he took a sip of his coffee.

"Come on, Mark. Come over and eat. I don't expect small talk or a deep conversation out of you. Just eat some food," Julie said insistently.

"I'm sorry, but I can't. Not tonight. Thanks for the offer though," Mark said stubbornly.

"Are you sure? Nick will be home and if you want to talk about anything-" Julie continued.

"Julie, I said no. Please understand. I have things to do," he was becoming short with her. He didn't want to be rude, but he really didn't want to be social right now, let alone go to someone's house for dinner.

"Oh, okay. I understand," Julie said, looking down.

"Damn. Why did she have to be so nice?" Mark thought. He hated to disappoint her.

"Is it anything that I could help you with? You know, you don't even have to ask, just tell me what needs to be done. I could call some family-" Julie was cut off mid-sentence.

"No, it's nothing like that. But thanks anyway," he said frankly.

"Are you sure? I could go to the grocery store or…"

"Yes! Julie, I'm sure," Marks loud and impatient voice came as shock to him. He toned it down immediately.

"There's nothing for you to do, there's no family to call, just… don't worry about it. If I need help, I'll ask for it," he leaned onto the counter top, sliding down onto his elbows and rubbing his head with both hands. Mark took a deep breath and slowly exhaled. He looked over at a silent Julie.

She stared at him with wide watery eyes. "I'm sorry, I didn't mean to upset you. I was just trying to help," her voice trembled.

"Aw, shit, I'm sorry," Mark felt bad. Realizing his overreaction, he went over and sat across from her. Mark reached out and grabbed her hand, giving her a half smile.

"I'm sorry, Jules, I know you're just trying to help me out. The kinds of stuff I need to get done are only things I can handle. It's nothing personal, it's just…. complicated. Okay? You're very nice and helpful, but I need some time right now to sort out my own issues. Please, understand that it has nothing to do with you," Mark explained his current situation the best he could.

Julie looked up at him and sensed his frustration. "Of course, I understand. I mean, I guess I do," she tried to put her fragile emotions aside.

"Have you heard anything from the police or the Doctors yet?" She asked.

"No. Not yet, but I'm… um… never mind," Mark paused.

She was confused by the strange vibes he was giving off. Mark was acting… well, NOT like Mark.

Mark wondered if he should say something to her about hiring Williams to investigate Allie's death. He suddenly wanted to tell her… everything. But, what would he say? How would he explain it?

(I'm not the man you and Nick think I am. Allie's death wasn't an accident. You're in possible danger just being my friend and especially being here in my house.) Mark thought that this might be a little too much for her to handle right now. "Not the right time," he thought.

Mark glanced at her face, but lingered for a moment. She was a very beautiful woman, even when she was upset and on the verge of crying. She's a good friend, he'd say to himself, whenever he thought of her in this way. However, there was no denying that they had always had this… chemistry. The very first time they'd met, they couldn't stop smiling at each other, for no apparent reason. He had to force himself not to smile or look at her just to keep others from noticing. Mark quickly realized that he shouldn't be thinking about his friend and coworker's wife this way.

He drank down the rest of his black coffee and went to the sink, setting his cup inside. His phone got a text and vibrated just then. He turned his back to pull it out of his pocket and read it. It was from Williams.

"Mark, are you okay? Did you find something out from the Doctor?" Julie was still waiting on his answer. She was concerned with his weird behavior.

"I'm still waiting to hear from the investigating detectives, but the Doctor last night said it could be a few things. A food allergy, or cross contamination. They said that she most likely "asphyxiated," he paused. He hated the sound of that word.

Julie gasped. "Oh, my... so it was something she ate? Like an allergic reaction to her dinner or something? That doesn't make any sense," she said.

"Yeah, I guess. A food handling accident of some kind, whatever the hell that means, but we won't know anything till later on this week.   So, it's a waiting game," Mark took a deep breath and glanced at Julie.

"Look, I'm being a little impatient, I know. I'm really sorry, but I'm on edge right now. I'm not the best company, so... if you don't mind," Mark looked down at the counter, hoping she would get the hint and understand that he was trying to tell her... to leave.

"Yeah, that's fine. It's more than fine, it's totally fine!" She nervously waved her hand. "No need to apologize for anything. Least of all, how your feeling," her voice was shaking.

"I hope you get all the answers you need really soon, and that you get all your, uh... stuff done, that you need to get done today or whatever," she stood up from the table, nervously grabbing at her purse.

Mark reached across the table to pick up her coffee mug and Julie grabbed it. "I can get it, Mark," she snapped.

His warm hand covered hers and lingered. Julie froze. She looked up into his eyes. What seemed like a totally innocent and accidental gesture became something more. There was that connection, that unmistakable spark. Their bodies were so close, that they inhaled the same breath the other exhaled. It was, as if they were breathing life into each other.

He cleared his throat and looked away, letting go of her hand.

She quickly went to the sink and rinsed out her cup, setting it onto the counter.

"I've got to get going anyway, dinner doesn't cook itself," she fidgeted with her purse on her shoulder as she went to the door. Her hands shook as she fumbled with the handle.

"It's locked. Let me get that for you," Mark reached around her and unlocked the door. He stepped out and looked around before holding the door open for her.

"Thanks for stopping by, Julie. I appreciate it," Mark said to her as she got into her car.

"No problem. Will we be seeing you at 5:30? It is meatloaf night, don't turn me down!" She raised her eyebrows and gave him a sympathetic look.

"Julie, I already told you, I can't-" he started to protest, but she stopped him.

"If you don't come, I'll understand. But the offer is still there."

She pointed her finger at him, gave him a stern look and said, "Don't start holding your feelings in and alienating yourself from people who care about you, it isn't healthy. You know you can talk to me anytime, about anything, day or night. Besides, the last thing you want is to bottle it all up. You'll only end up lashing out and hurting someone," Julie said seriously.

He nodded and waved as she backed down the driveway leading to the back alley.

"If you only knew," Mark said to himself. He walked to the end of the lane and watched her drive away.

CHAPTER 7

WELL-MADE TABLES

"Hello, Mr. Anderson," Williams sounded glad that Mark had called him back so quickly.

"Good evening Detective Williams. I got your text, saying we could speak in the morning, but I was wondering if we could talk now. Do you have a minute?" He asked.

Mark didn't care too much for texting. Unless it was a quick message, he just preferred a regular phone call. He was "old school" is what Allie would say.

"Yes, of course," Williams said. "Now is just fine."

"Were you able to find out anything from the prison today?" Mark put his phone on speaker and sat it on the bathroom counter.

Wiping the steam off the mirror, he looked at himself for the first time since he'd lost her. He could almost hear her scolding him for taking too hot a shower.

"The steam isn't good for the paint on the walls, Dad. Plus, the heat can dry your skin out too. At least crack a window!" She would say. What he wouldn't give to hear her nagging him again.

"Are you still there, Mark, or did I lose you?" Williams asked.

"Yeah, Sorry, I'm still here. What do you got?" Mark refocused on the conversation.

"I got a name off of the visitors log for Mr. Vanzetti," He stated proudly.

Taking his phone off speaker, Mark held it between his ear and shoulder. He walked to his dresser and picked up a pen.

"There's just one name? Okay, what is it?" He found an old receipt lying on top, flipped it over and waited for Williams to begin.

"You know what, I'm only about five minutes from your house. Would you prefer if I just stopped by? I thought you might want to take a look at the print out I have," Williams asked.

"Yes, actually, that would be better," Mark sounded surprised. "Five minutes then?"

"Yep, see you soon," Williams concluded.

Mark hung up the phone and quickly finished dressing. He slid his gun holsters over his shoulders and secured it under his arms. Mark secured his loaded pistols inside and snapped it together across his chest, carefully concealing them under his leather jacket.

"Who's been visiting you Leo? Who in this world would care about you?" Mark mumbled to himself as he walked down the hall and made his way down the stairs.

Talking out loud made him feel like someone else was there… like he wasn't completely alone in that big empty house.

Mark suddenly remembered Julie and checked the time. It was after 6:00 p.m. Mark text Julie, saying, "Running late start without me," she text him back with, "No dice," he almost smiled on that one.

Hearing a car pull up outside, he walked over and stood next to the back door. The motion light by the back door came on. He carefully peeked out the side of the curtain to make sure it was Williams before he opened the door to greet him.

~

"Nick, are you still on the phone with work?" Julie slowly opened the door to the dimly lit den and knocked on the door frame. "He's been on the phone long enough," she thought. "If it's that important he should've stayed at work. He can be home for ten minutes, it's not going to kill him."

She peeked inside and couldn't see him at the desk. The sun was setting and there weren't any lamps on. Suddenly, she heard his voice, out on the veranda that was connected to the den. She pushed the door open wider. Julie walked into the den, slowly making her way through the shadows, towards the open French doors. Suddenly, she heard his voice. He was outside on the porch leaning against the wood railing… whispering harshly into his phone.

"I have a very good reason to be freaking out! I don't think you quite understand how hard this is for me! I'm supposed to be his friend for God's sake! Now he's asking questions and all kinds of shit," Nick seemed frantic, almost scared. There was a long pause, but Julie continued to listen.

"I don't know what he said to the damn detective!! AND… to top it all off, my stupid wife has invited him HERE… for dinner, tonight!" He was clutching his cell phone hard, and practically spitting on it.

Julie froze. Her body felt strangely heavy all of the sudden. Who was he talking to like that? And who is he calling stupid? She backed up into the wall and stood as still as she could. Her eyes squinted as she tried to focus harder on listening.

"Alright…okay! I'll stay and see what I can find out. Don't worry, I can do it… I don't really have a choice, do I? I'll see you tomorrow… you too," he said in a calmer tone.

Julie panicked, realizing that he was about to hang up. He would walk in and surely see her standing there. She needed to get out, and fast. She walked back towards the door as quickly and quietly as she could, hoping he wouldn't think she overheard his call. Instead, she stopped just before running out the door and switched on the light instead.

"Honey, are you out there?" She bellowed loudly as she turned around and walked swiftly back toward the balcony.

"Yeah, I'm right here," Nick was startled. He shut the French doors behind him and walked into the den. "I was just finishing up a phone call," Nick said quickly.

"Oh, that was a long one. What was that all about?" Julie asked innocently.

"I have a meeting at the restaurant tomorrow morning… just had to go over some things," Nick said, believably enough.

He flashed a quick smile and took a swig off the beer he held in his hand. "I didn't want to bore you with it in the kitchen! I decided that I'm going to stay home and have dinner with you tonight, regardless of what's going on at the restaurant. They're just going to have to get along without me," Nick's demeanor changed and he seemed very convincing.

"Great, are you almost ready to eat?" She smiled.

"Absolutely, I'm ready when you are," Nick said overly excitedly.

"Mark is running a little late, but he'll be here soon." Julie was surprised at how calm and nonchalant her voice sounded. Her hand was steady, as her husband took it and led her into the dining room.

~

Mark sat at the kitchen table with Williams. He looked over copy of the prisons "Visitor Sign-in Roster" that Williams handed him.

"Christina L. Mazzo?" Mark was puzzled. "Do we know who she is, yet?"

"I don't know yet, there is absolutely NO record of her. Not even a speeding ticket. I was hoping you could tell me," Williams said.

Mark concentrated and shook his head.

"Well, whoever she is, she's been visiting him regularly, twice actually, just this last month. I'm assuming she's local to visit him so often in New Jersey," he looked at Mark. "So, the name doesn't ring a bell with you, at all?" Williams felt a little let down. He was excited to show Mark what he was able to get.

"No, not at all," Mark rubbed the back of his neck and leaned back in the chair. "Maybe she's someone he met thru another inmate? Or, could be a wife or girlfriend of someone he already knows."

Williams commented. "Maybe she's his girlfriend."

"Maybe, they could be using the woman as a front to relay messages," Mark thought out loud. Mark looked up at the ceiling as his mind ran the idea one more time.

"Get her to sign in, be on camera, and then talk business thru the glass," Williams was trying to wrap his head around the notion.

"That would appear innocent enough," he decided.

"That's it. We got it!" Mark exclaimed.

"What's that?" Williams inquired.

"The surveillance cameras," Mark sat up in his chair. "There's got to be security footage, right? Maybe we can I.D. her that way."

"Nice, I can get us that first thing tomorrow morning. I'll do the best I can, giving that it's a Sunday," Williams felt hopeful again.

"The guys over there don't have anything exciting to do anyway," Mark added. "So, let's do it. In the meantime, could you make a call to your department and run that last name against the other inmates, just in case there's a connection?" Mark said.

Williams nodded in agreement. "Yeah, I can do that."

"I appreciate your work. Thank you," Mark stood and shook his hand.

"Let's meet tomorrow morning at the coffee shop on the corner of 6th and Main. Eight o'clock," Mark opened the back door. "I'll walk you out."

"That sounds good to me, Mark. See you tomorrow morning," Williams said as he walked to his car.

Mark walked back into the house, locked the door and shut off the lights. Leaning up against the wall, he peeked out the back window. That's when he saw the black Ford Expedition. It slowly pulled out behind Williams as he drove away. It was too slow to be tailing him, probably just keeping an eye on him and verifying his whereabouts. It was a precinct vehicle… unmarked. He knew it was only a matter of time before they got curious.

Mark zipped up his jacket and went out the front door, locking it behind him. It was about a ten minute walk to Nick and Julies. He welcomed the crisp cool air on his face and the crunching of dead leaves under his boots as he walked down the sidewalk. It was definitely autumn, Allies favorite season. All though she would say it was "fall", because, the leaves "fall from the trees, Daddy", a then seven year old Allie had explained. Thinking back now… maybe raking the leaves wasn't the worst chore after all. As long as he had Allie there to jump in them and mess up his neatly raked piles, he would gladly do it every day.

His chest tightened up as he drew in a cold, ragged breath; his head began to pound. He felt sick to his stomach. Mark had hardly slept, and didn't have an appetite. Maybe he would drink some coffee, but that would be about it. He had no desire for any sustenance at all.

The stress he was under was starting to take a physical toll on him. It served as a reminder that his body was still alive and trying to function normally, even if his mind wasn't.

Marks dilemma was that he couldn't bear to think of his daughter as being dead, it would debilitate him. He almost couldn't believe that she wasn't here with him, now. It just wasn't real to him sometimes, but despite his rejection, it was painfully obvious that she really was gone.

It was getting easier for him to block the idea from his mind whenever it became devastatingly apparent that this was, in fact, his reality.

Mark stayed focused on keeping his body moving. Step after step, breathing in and out, and keeping his eyes open and alert. He didn't know how to pretend that he wasn't anything other than a hollowed man with nothing left to lose. But he would try to act sociable tonight, for Julie. She needed this, and if it would make her happy, than he would be there.

Mark also struggled with the decision on whether to tell Nick and Julie about everything. He decided that despite Nick's odd behavior lately, he trusted them enough to tell them about his past. They were two of his only friends and they would understand. After all, they had lost her too. Everyone needed to hear the truth.

~

Mark sat full and satisfied, admiring the large oak table where the three of them now sat. Bright red drapes served as the back drop behind Nick and Julie. The color matched the table cloth that he ran his hands over.

"Well-made table," he commented aloud, "Good size too."

Mark could smell the apple pie that now cooled in the other room. He felt a small pang of guilt. It was amazing that he ate dinner, let alone contemplated eating a slice of pie. Allie couldn't have any apple pie… not anymore. She would have had hers with a scoop of vanilla ice cream on top. "Allie-mode," she always said.

"Hey man, are you all right?" Nick was looking at him, wide eyed and concerned.

Mark stopped day dreaming and looked up at them. Julie was staring at him in utter disbelief. She was speechless and hadn't said a word the entire time. Mark had drifted off in thought for a moment, and had briefly forgotten that he had just told them his entire life story.

"Oh my gosh, Mark," Julie finally said. She put her hands on her forehead and rubbed her temple. "You have been through so much. And poor Allie... she had no idea, did she?" Julie wiped her teary eyes.

"She remembered Aunt Alice... but not a whole lot more. If she did, she never let on. We didn't talk about it at all. We just moved on and started living a different life... until now," Mark stated.

"So, is that why you hired that detective from the other night?" Nick asked. "You think this Leo guy had something to do with it?"

Marks gaze switched from Julie to Nick. He suspiciously glared at Nick through narrowed eyes.

"What makes you so sure that I hired a detective?" Mark asked.

"Oh, I don't know for sure if you did. I just saw you talking to him that night at the restaurant…that's all," he said nervously.

"Well, you see, Nick, when someone's usually healthy daughter mysteriously dies, the police usually have a few questions for people. They call those cops… Homicide Detectives," Mark said sarcastically.

"Well, yeah. I know that, but you were talking to him for a while and it would make sense if you did hire him, for extra investigating, especially after what you just told us," Nick tried to justify his unusual statement.

"I mean, Wow! My mind is just blown right now man… you sure have been through a lot! I'm really sorry to hear that that happened to you and… Allie," Nick said nervously trying to seem sympathetic.

"So you think that if I'm having a conversation with the Detective, that I must have hired him for a side job?" Mark was pushing him for more of a response. Nick shouldn't have known about Detective Williams being hired, at all.

"Well, yeah, no… I mean, I guess not," he was back peddling. "So what do you think happened? You know, to Allie, or Lily, I mean," he was shifting in his seat to get more comfortable.

Mark winced at hearing Nick call Allie by her real name. The conversation quickly became more intense.

Julie was watching Nick. She must have thought he was acting strange, too.

"I don't know what happened. That's probably why I hired the Detective, right Nick?" Mark said dryly.

Julie was confused by the negative turn the conversation took.

"Okay, guys. I know this is a lot to take in all at once. Please, excuse Nick; his manners are horrible lately...I don't think he slept a wink last night either," Julie tried to diffuse the uncomfortable situation.

"Oh? You're not sleeping well, Nick? I wonder why that is," Mark intentionally intimidated him now.

Nick was about to say something, but Julie put her hand up... shaking her head at Nick.

"No, really, I'm so sorry to hear that," Mark said sarcastically. "You must be really stressed out with all the added responsibilities at work and all."

Julie sat up straight and stared harshly at Mark.

"Look, I think I know what the "raised emotions" are about and you don't have to worry, Mark," Julie said. Her blue eyes softened as she continued. "We're more than just your friends here we're like family and there's no need to be so defensive. We will support anything you're doing. We're here for you when you need us, alright? End of story...we're not the enemy," she took a drink of her wine and sat back into her chair. Obviously exhausted, she rubbed her eyes.

Putting himself in check, Mark nodded and looked at them both. "Thank you, for your friendship and your understanding," he looked at Nick as he spoke. "It means a lot right now."

Nick swallowed, hard.

Julie continued.

"You're very welcome. Seriously though, if you suspect this guy Leo, has something to do with Allie's death, can't you just go to witness protection and have them investigate it? Surely someone else might suspect this Leo Vanzetti's involvement, given the history this dirt bag has, especially with your family! Plus, he's getting out on Monday? It just seems so cut and dry," Julie exclaimed.

Mark was glad to hear someone else say what he has felt all along. "You would think so, but it's being treated as a complete coincidence. I've already been told by my witness protection coordinator, that there's no way "Mr. Vanzetti" has anything to do with it. He has a solid alibi I mean, he's in prison until his parole hearing on Monday morning. So, yes, that's why I'm pursuing this on my own and I hired Detective Williams. I'll be meeting him tomorrow at Allie's favorite coffee shop," Mark looked at Nick, who now looked very worried.

"I know that they don't see the situation as I do, and I can't prove anything right now, anyway. I just want to uncover the truth, and put whoever is responsible, behind bars," he took a drink of his now cold coffee and shot a glare at Nick. Why was his friend acting so sketchy?

"No kidding!" Nick blurted out. "What kind of fucking sicko would want to poison a little girl anyway? I hope you get all the proof you need, man," Nick was rocking back and forth in his wooden chair, causing it to creak loudly with every jerking motion. Julie noticed again, how weird her husband was acting. That wasn't a rocking chair.

Mark had to admit, he was slightly entertained by Nick, picking up on this awkward outburst. Mark had suspected that he was on drugs for a while, and this just proved him right. After all, Mark used to be a narcotics agent. He hadn't said anything to Dom, let alone Julie, but with him acting out like this, it shouldn't be hard for them to figure it out on their own.

"Thanks, Nick, but we don't know for sure if she was "poisoned". We won't know anything until after the autopsy is performed. Dom is just as anxious, he's scheduled it for me as early as possible after this long holiday weekend," Mark mentioned.

The sudden image of Allie's cold body flashed in his mind.

"I keep seeing her… all laid out in her pretty dress with her brown curly hair all fanned out like a little porcelain doll," Marks eyes clouded over with darkness as he stared off again.

Julie's body shuddered as she too, remembered the image of Allie in the triage unit.

Nicks face turned white as he listened to Mark and noticed Julie's body language.

"Nick, why don't you go get desert for us," Julie suddenly suggested. She gestured to the kitchen with a nod of her head.

"Yeah, sure, I'll be back in a few minutes. I need to go use the bathroom anyway," Nick said. He got up from the table, tripping over his feet. Finding his footing, he turned and made his way into the kitchen.

She watched hesitantly as Nick left the room.

Julie quickly turned, leaned in and whispered to Mark, "I need to talk to you about Nick! It's important, Mark. Just trust me on this. Do you trust me?" She asked, shaking.

"Yes, I do," Mark answered softly.

"Something is wrong; very "off" with him… for quite some time now," she looked at the closed kitchen door. "I think it has to do with you and your story!" She was very frightened.

"Okay, Calm down Jules. Just keep it together for a little while longer. He smiled at her and it seemed to give her some reassurance. "I know exactly what you mean," Mark confirmed.

She nodded, then straightened herself up and cleared her throat. He heard Nick flush the toilet in the hall bathroom.

"Do you remember where I said I was meeting Detective Williams tomorrow morning?" Mark asked.

"Allie's favorite coffee shop," Julie said quietly. She remembered, and knew just where to go.

"Meet me there at eight o'clock," he silently mouthed the words.

Julie nodded and sat back into her chair.

Mark slowly pushed his chair from the table as the chair scraped loudly on the floor.

"I'm going to get us some coffee to go with that pie," Mark said loudly.

"No need for that, I got it right here!" Nick exclaimed. He came banging thru the doors into the dining room carrying the pie and a decanter of hot coffee. "Sorry about that wait!"

Julie managed to smile at her husband as he poured her a cup of coffee and sat it next to her dessert plate.

"Thank you, my friend, I definitely appreciate it," Mark grinned and held up his coffee cup.

"No, problem, and like Jule's said, if there's anything we can do, just let us know," Nick tried to look sincere as he poured Marks coffee, but his weakened voice betrayed him.

~

That night, as Mark walked home he thought about Nick. Was it his imagination playing tricks on him, or could his old friend know something about what happened to Allie? Despite being an obvious crack head, could there be another reason for his odd behavior? One thing was evident. Nick didn't seem surprised at all to hear about his secret past. That could only mean one of two things. Either, he was so shocked the only way he could respond was with awkward questioning, or Nick was no stranger to the story. He had heard it before.

Mark thought that from this point on, he had to question everything about the "safe new life" he thought he was living, including, his relationships with the people in it.

Nick's behavior at the restaurant lately was erratic and his work ethic had been dwindling away the last six months or so. He acted like he just didn't care anymore. Mark tried to stay out of Dom's business, but he had had to go to him about Nick a few times. You just never knew which Nick you were dealing with at any given time. Nice, funny, laid back Nick, or loud, snappy and ticked off Nick. You just can't be like that working with the public, especially in the hospitality business. It wasn't ever personal at all… but he had a feeling it was about to get that way.

CHAPTER 8

THE OFFICE

Mark and Detective Williams had already begun to drink their coffee, when Mark spotted Julie coming through the door. Seeming quite winded, her blue frightened eyes searched the busy coffee shop for a familiar face.

Mark stood to get her attention and gestured with his hand, "Over here."

"Thank you, for letting me intrude upon your meeting. I had to talk to you as soon as possible," she said to Mark, looking hesitantly at Detective Williams.

"Not a problem, Jules. You're not intruding. Don't worry about the detective, you can trust him," Mark assured her. "I do."

Mark introduced them and they sat down at the table at the back of the noisy café. With so much noise and chatter, there was no danger of being overheard. A young man walked up in an apron and placed a 'to-go' cup of hot herbal tea in front of Julie. Mark had ordered it shortly before she arrived.

"Thank you," Julie was flattered.

She was pleasantly surprised by this small act of kindness. Nick wouldn't have ordered anything for her. He didn't even know she drank tea. She took a cautious sip and smiled at Mark. It calmed her down a little bit.

"Do you feel comfortable telling us both what the matter is, Julie?" Mark was inquisitive.

Julie nodded and took another sip of her tea before she began.

"I overheard Nick's phone call last evening," she looked at Mark. "It seemed like he was talking about you. Almost like he had been following you or something and whoever he was speaking to, was telling him what to do and for him to calm down. He said that he had to meet whoever it was at the restaurant today."

Mark could tell that she was focusing very hard on saying exactly what she had heard.

"He was very upset, and kept saying he didn't know what to do and how he's supposed to be your friend, and then he called me stupid," she was talking faster now and was becoming upset.

"Ok, it's alright. Do you know who he was talking to?" Mark asked.

She shook her head no. "I don't have the slightest clue! He just told me it had something to do with work, but he could be lying."

"All I know, is he is meeting or (has met) with this mystery person at the restaurant, sometime today and they will apparently make his situation all better," she was visibly shaking.

"He said, "I'm starting to freak, this is getting hard for me, I'm supposed to be his friend, he's asking questions, my stupid wife invited him over" and then it switched to.. "Alright, I've got this. Don't worry, see you tomorrow," she animatedly spoke with her hands.

"Do you think this means that he has something to do with Allie's death?" Julie clasped her hand over mouth, afraid of what she had just said. She quickly lowered her head, and wiped away the tears.

"It's going to be alright. I'm not real sure what this means, but we'll figure it out," Mark whispered to her. He shot a glance at Williams.

"Oh, my gosh! I hate to think such horrible things, but this is over the top for him. He hasn't been himself in almost a year, and we barely talk. We don't even sleep in the same bed anymore. We only ACT like a married couple… and now this?" Julie hesitated. "I filed for divorce about 3 months ago. He hasn't signed the papers yet. I thought we would try to work things out, but that's not it. He wants to wait to sign, and I'm not sure why."

Julie shook her head and closed her eyes. "I knew that wasn't going to happen smoothly. He knows I'm not in love him anymore. He's become a stranger, Mark. I don't even know who he is anymore or what he's capable of doing," she grabbed a napkin and quickly swiped her cheeks.

"I had no idea things were so bad between you, Jules. I'm sorry," Mark tried to console her, but all he could think of was Nick, and where he might be right now.

Williams glanced at Mark now. They knew they were thinking the same thing. Nick's odd behavior told them all that he was definitely hiding something. Especially, by the way he had acted last night. Mark had already told Williams about it.

"Thank you Mrs. Butler, for telling us what you heard. I know it's not easy for you, but we appreciate your help," Williams was trying to calm her.

"Do your best to act normal around him Jules, and go to work as usual. Try to put this out of your mind. I'll do my best to find out what's going on, alright?" Mark patted her hand.

"Okay. I will try," Julie said nervously. She felt a little out of place suddenly and decided it was time to leave.

She grabbed her purse and slid the strap over her shoulder, hugging it close to her body for comfort.

"I'll talk to you as soon as I know something. You're a good friend Jule's. Thanks for coming to me about this," Mark and Detective Williams stood and said goodbye to Julie.

Mark decided that he would walk Julie to the door and see her out, but just as they made their way towards the exit, Mark began to hear Williams' phone ring. Williams motioned to Mark that he would be staying at the table. He had been anticipating this phone call.

A few moments later, after saying goodbye to Julie, Mark walked back to the table, where he saw Williams hang up his phone. Immediately, he looked serious. Mark remained standing.

"That was my Captain, Mark. He wants us to come by, to tell you about something we've discovered," Williams said, reluctantly.

"What do you mean something "we've" discovered? You told your Captain?" Mark was blindsided.

"I'm sorry, Mark. I had no choice. I had to tell my Captain what was going on, he was having me followed. My job was on the line, I mean, I'm not a private investigator, I had to explain. He thought that my involvement with the case was beginning to exceed the normalcies of a homicide investigation, so I had to tell him about the connection. I'm sorry Mark, but he's promised to keep it to himself, and he's also stopped the tail he had on me. You can trust him…and you can still trust me. He can help us," Williams was very sincere and was deeply sorry for breaking his promise of anonymity to Mark.

Mark was considering this. He had to think very carefully

about the Captains involvement. Maybe he could use this as an opportunity. Whether he trusted the Captain or not…he could use him to get information he wouldn't normally have. There was nothing he could really do about it now.

"I don't really have a choice, do I?" Mark didn't like the idea, but in the end it's not going to matter anyway. If there were dirty cops involved, it wouldn't be a major surprise. If the Captain was legit, then it would definitely help to have all their support and contacts. Anything to get him closer to Leo…

"I know you don't like the idea, but this is the best thing for everyone. You want answers right, proof? He can help. I think we should really head over now. Are you going to follow me over, or would you like a ride?"   Williams said as pulled out his keys.

Mark looked at his watch. "I'll ride with you, I walked this morning."

"It's nine o'clock," Mark thought. "I wonder where Nick is."

~

Julie had an overwhelming feeling of dread as she drove back to work. She didn't know if it was fear or adrenaline that fueled it. She knew her husband was up to no good, and she felt compelled to get an explanation. Tires squealing, Julie abruptly turned the car around and drove to the restaurant.

She parked in the back lot of a department store, hoping her car wouldn't be recognized. It was just across the alley, from the restaurants back parking lot. She pulled the hood of her jacket over her head.

"It's show time Jule's," she said to herself. Julie walked across the parking lot, and headed towards the service entrance of the restaurant. She saw Nicks truck, and tried to pay close attention to the few other vehicles, but who was she kidding? She didn't know which people drove what, anyway!

Suddenly, the metal doors swung open and hit the building with a loud bang, startling Julie out of her mind. A man carrying linen bags came out, instantly apologizing for the scare.

"Hello, there! My husband works here... Nick Butler? Could you hold the door for me?" She asked sweetly.

"Oh, yes, Mrs. Butler, go on in! He's in Dom's office I believe," he said with a warm smile.

She thanked him and wished him a great day. She needed to refocus on the task at hand. She didn't know exactly what to say to Nick, but she would figure something out. She was determined to get answers.

A young lady stood in the dining hall arranging the table settings, when Julie came walking out of the kitchen. She looked up from her silverware and noticed Julie.

"Hello, Miss, can I help you?" She asked as she began to walk towards her.

"Hi! I'm Julie Butler, Nick's wife," Julie said.

"Oh, yes. Hello! My name is Sophia. I'm Dom's niece, Anita's daughter," she smiled.

Julie walked over to her and shook her hand. "It's a pleasure to meet you, I'm sorry to hear that your mother is ill," Julie said sincerely.

"Thank you," she said quietly. She smiled warmly at Julie. Julie had never heard of Sophia before.

"I'm looking for my husband, is he in your Uncle's office?" Julie began to walk towards the hallway.

"Yes, I believe so, but he's in a meeting right now. Would you like to wait out here?" Sophia began to walk after her.

"No, that's alright. I'll see him now, thanks," Julie reached the hallway, continuing towards the office.

"But he's with my Aunt, and I have specific orders that they are not to be disturbed," Sophia said persistently.

Julie stopped and turned towards Sophia, "Your Aunt …Lucy?" Julie quickly turned back around and walked even faster and as she came up to the office, she could still hear Sophia's protests.

"Please, Miss Julie, you will get me in so much trouble!" She whispered harshly.

Julie got to the door and stopped abruptly, with Sophia quick on her heels. Julie quickly turned and faced her, putting a finger to her own lips to silence the girl. Listening to the muffled conversation on the other side of the door, Julie was able to discern the two voices. Only able to make out certain words, she leaned in closer and focused harder.

"You guys are going to protect me, right? You won't let all this come back on me?" Nick was frantic.

"Don't worry so much!" Lucy said. "Everything's going to work out, just as planned. You need to calm down and keep it together for just one more day. Do you think you can handle THAT?" Lucy's annoyance was obvious.

"Keep your wits about you, your acting like an idiot!" Lucy's tone was icy.

"I'm sorry, I'm trying! It's just that I'll feel better once he gets here and I know everything's cool between us," Nick said. Julie heard Nick plop down into Dom's squeaky leather chair.

"Trust me, Darling. He will be grateful for all you've done for us. As soon as he gets here tomorrow, you will be properly rewarded," Lucy lowered and softened her voice.

"Until then, Lover, you shouldn't worry about pleasing anyone… but me." Julie heard what sounded like a moan from Nick. The sound of crinkling papers and the squeaky chair told her ears more than she needed to know. Lucy began to giggle.

It became incredibly clear that there was something going on between them. Julie's stomach churned and she covered her mouth. Stumbling back down the hallway with Sophia at her side,

Julie turned and pointed in the office's direction.

"Don't you dare tell them I was here, you got it?" Julie scolded.

Sophia nodded, but Julie didn't see. She was already out of the kitchen and had bolted out the back door, sprinting across the parking lot. Just before she made it to her car… Julie stopped, and vomited in a bush.

CHAPTER 9

THINK FAST

Mark and Detective Williams were seated in Captain Jack Haddock's office. After meeting him, Mark had to admit, he seemed like an alright guy. Mark wasn't paying any attention to Williams and Haddock's conversation, as it didn't pertain to him. Mark was looking at the pictures of his wife and children on his desk. They seemed like a very happy family, even if they happened to be smiling for the sake of their pictures.

"Nice, bright smiles," Mark said aloud. "What are their names?" Mark asked.

"Pardon me?" Captain Haddock looked puzzled. He glanced at Williams then back to Mark.

"The names of your family," Mark answered.

"Oh! That's my wife, Patricia, and our four children, Natalie, Michael, Amanda and Jack Haddock Jr.," he smiled proudly.

"Lovely family, congratulations," Mark said politely.

"Thank you, Mr. Anderson," said Haddock.

He wasn't sure what to say to Mark, if he should say anything at all. Maybe something along the lines of… "I'm sorry to hear about your family, sorry they've all passed?" No, he decided. That wouldn't be appropriate.

There was an uncomfortable silence in the air.

"Sir, you said you had information regarding the woman who had visited Mr. Vanzetti?" Williams asked, breaking the awkward tension and bringing up business at hand as the topic of conversation, once again.

"Awe, yes! I received a photo that you requested from a security camera at the prison. I was also able to get another name, an alias, when we ran Christina L. Mazzo against a missing person's data base," Haddock stated.

"Missing persons?" Mark asked.

"Apparently, Christina L. Mazzo… simply disappeared one afternoon, after telling her husband that she was going for a walk, poor fellow," Haddock added.

Haddock opened a file that had been in front of him. "All though it seems to me, that Christina L. Mazzo is the alias," he took a long drink of his coffee, finishing it.

"Really," Williams was fascinated. "Then what's her real

name?" he asked.

Haddock handed Williams the print out, as Mark anxiously grabbed the photo. Williams began to read aloud….

"Christina L. Mazzo, a.k.a. Christina Lucia Vanzetti… is the only known living relative…" Williams's voice faded as he looked up and noticed Marks reaction to the photo he held.

Mark's grip tightened, crinkling the paper print out and bundling it up in his fist. He placed it in front of the unsuspecting Williams to look at it. Mark sat back down swiftly, and fell forward, putting his head in his hands.

"Christina Lucia Vanzetti is Leo's older sister!" Mark said. He stood straight up out of his chair, causing it to fall backwards.

Williams reached up to grab Marks trembling shoulder, and stop him from leaving, "Ok, calm down Mark, at least we know who she is now. Did you know her personally?" he asked.

Mark looked up at the ceiling, put his hands behind his head and smiled eerily. Leaning over onto the desk, he slowly spoke to Haddock.

"Yeah, I knew her personally and I know who she is… NOW," Mark hissed.

He put his finger on the blurred black and white photo that lay half crumpled on the desk.

"Only I know her as, "Mrs. Lucy Angelo.""

~

Julie was too upset to be driving... but she felt like she needed to get far, far away. Her first thought was to go to the police and tell them what she had heard back at the restaurant, and tell them about the phone call she had overheard the night before. She had too many questions and not enough answers for them. To her, it was obvious that Nick was cheating on her, but that didn't matter to her now. She knew that they had grown distant over this last year... become different people even...but this?

To her it sounded like the impossible, that Nick might have actually done it. Nick might have killed Allie. If he did do it, who was it for... Lucy? NO, that made no sense. No sense at all! Her head was reeling. Then suddenly only one thing was clear. She had to find Mark and tell him...now. It would be very difficult to tell him such bad news, but she had to.

Julie pulled over at the busy gas station on the corner and parked. Dumping out the contents of her purse in the passenger seat, she easily found her cell phone, and called Mark.

"Mark, where are you?" she said out loud. It went straight to voice mail. He must have turned his phone off. She hung up not leaving a message. She decided to text him, "call a.s.a.p." Panic seized her stomach as she tried desperately to focus on what she needed to do next.

"One thing at a time, Jules," she whispered. She had to think fast. What if Sophia had already told them she was there? She would definitely have some explaining to do. She knew her life could very well be in danger if she told him that she knew everything... that she thought he had killed Allie and that she heard Lucy say, "Lover"...

That was it! Julie had a plan. May not be a good one, but it was a plan nonetheless. She could play the victim for a moment, if it meant keeping Nick and Lucy from wondering what she might have heard while she was there.

She took a deep breath and exhaled. "Okay, ASSHOLE. You want to play games... Let's play."

Julie picked up the phone and this time... she called Nick. Except, this time, he answered his phone right away. Damn! This threw her off, but only for a second.

"Hi! I came by the restaurant to see you, because I was thinking about how stressed you were about your meeting...and YOU were with LUCY in Dom's office. I want you to know, that I heard her call you Lover! LOVER, NICK! I didn't hear anything else... but that's all I needed to hear!" She sounded infuriated.

"Wait, Julie! Let me explain," Nick was panicking now.

"Don't expect me to be home when you get off work... and if you knew what was good for you, you'd let me cool off before you even TRY to contact me!" she growled.

"Ah, shit! Julie, I'm sorry! I never meant for you to find out this way-" Nick tried to apologize, but Julie hung up on him.

Shaking and half proud of herself... she now had a perfect

cover.

Julie immediately started driving towards the police station. They could at least help her get a hold of Detective Williams. And as for Nick, she had just busted him pretty good, that's all that was on his mind for now. He wouldn't be suspecting her of anything otherwise. She just bought herself some valuable time.

CHAPTER 10

UNARMED

There was a knock at the door to Captain Haddocks' office. The three men, on edge, stood as Deputy Hansen entered the room.

"Excuse me, Detective Williams. A Ms. Butler is here looking for you. She says it's pretty important," Deputy Hansen added. The Deputy gestured towards a woman sitting next to his desk.

"Julie?" Marks heart skipped a beat.

"Excuse me, Officer," Mark made his way around Deputy Hansen and went out the door towards Julie.

"Julie, what's the matter? What happened?" Mark was concerned to see his friend so visibly shaken and sitting in the police station.

Unable to actually tell him, there was so much going through her mind, she ran to him and hugged him tight. Just seeing him made her burst into tears. How was she supposed to get this all out? She had no idea where to begin.

"Please, come into my office," Captain Haddock held the door open.

Mark walked with Julie back into the Captains office and helped her into the chair where he was just sitting. He stood next to her, leaning back up against the wall. He was anxious to hear what she had to say.

Captain Haddock asked his Deputy, that they not be disturbed. He shut the door behind him.

With everyone listening closely, Julie began to tell them of her visit to the restaurant. She told them what she'd heard, and of her phone call to Nick. She explained how she used the claim of jealousy and rage to her advantage, to allow for time to speak with Williams. She spoke slowly, just trying to get it all out. It was very difficult for her. Haddock then asked Julie if she would agree to sign a statement, which she agreed to do, eagerly.

"I'll do anything that could possibly help," she said willingly.

"That was some quick thinking, Ms. Butler. You've done a great job," Haddock was very patient and sympathetic with her. "Is there anything we can get you? A bottle of water perhaps-"

Haddock was suddenly interrupted by a swift movement and a loud crash, as the door to his office had suddenly been torn from its hinges. A flurry of activity erupted in the precinct, outside of the now opened door. Mark was desperately trying to get out of the nearest exit, knocking over anything that was in his way. Detective Williams reacted quickly and ran after him. Another Officer saw this and managed to reach out and grab Mark's arm just as he went by his desk, but Mark skillfully twisted the man's arm back behind him and shoved him to the ground.

"Mark, STOP!" Williams yelled, lunging for him. He had managed to get his arms around Mark, and hang on, using his bodies "dead weight" to keep him from going any further. Mark spun his body, flinging Williams' to the ground.

"Mark, don't do this! Please stop!" Williams pleaded. He got up and ran after him again, jumping over a table and knocking papers and supplies onto the floor. He knew where Mark was headed. He was going after Nick.

Yelling for help, Williams shouted to the stunned officers. "Block the entrance! Don't let him leave!"

Other police officers began to grab at Mark and he fought them off too. One by one, they didn't stand a chance.

"He's unarmed!" Williams shouted.

Julie watched, horrified, from behind Captain Haddock, who stood in the shattered doorway.

"No, he's not Sir! He has two 9mm handguns strapped to his chest!" Deputy Hansen exclaimed.

Williams paused. He honestly didn't know that. Five officers descended upon Mark.

"Just let me go!" he growled.

One of them kicked his legs out from under him as they struggled to get Mark onto his stomach. They managed to get his arms twisted behind him to handcuff him. He continued to resist as they pressed his face harder into the floor. Mark suddenly felt a shocking pain in the side of his neck, as volts of electricity pulsed through his body, temporarily paralyzing him. They stripped him of his guns.

Williams suddenly appeared over him, telling the officers to get up. "You got him down, now hand him over to me. Come on; get off him … NOW!"

Haddock tried to explain to his men what was going on.

"He just found out, that it might have been his friend that killed his daughter. Please, restrain him, but give him the benefit of the doubt. He's a grieving father," Haddock tried to diffuse the suddenly volatile situation.

Marks ridged body jolted on the floor. He continued to fight, even with the effects of the second dose of the Taser coursing through him. Williams knelt down next to Mark's head and breathlessly tried to calm him.

"Now is not the time for revenge. Just try to hold on to that last little bit of sanity you got. I know it's there somewhere. Let us bring Nick in and question him. You can trust me, okay? Stop fighting us and they'll remove the taser."

Williams tried to catch his breath and sat down on the floor. Mark stopped moving and lay still on the floor.

"We can't just let you go and kill someone, even if he does deserve it. We'll get him, and when we do, you bet your ass, you'll be there to see it," Williams stayed next to him and waved off the other police officers that stood nearby. He decided to wait a moment before he would un-cuff Mark. Mark didn't say a word.

Williams helped Mark, as he struggled to sit up. He looked like he was in a lot of pain. Williams removed the barbs from his neck. Marks red face was distorted, but not by the sting of the Taser. It was pure anger and turmoil. His icy glare was dark as night. Inside, the ominous betrayal that he felt burned into his very soul.

Mark let out a stifled roar, like a beast being gutted alive. Trying to lean over towards the waste basket, he dry heaved several times. His guts constricted and squeezed him from the inside out.

He clamped his eyes shut, and just like every other time he tried to close them, he saw his daughter, cold and un-breathing. Her eyes would never open again.

The feelings and emotions that he had pushed aside over the last 48 hours…began to surface. Tears streamed down his face as he choked back the uncontrollable sobs. He couldn't suppress it anymore.

With both hands, Williams gripped Mark's shoulders again, but this time it wasn't to restrain his friend, it was to support him. The other officers slowly wandered to another part of the station. No one said anything. They didn't quite know what to say or do.

They just stared at the floor…and listened, as Mark finally began to grieve.

~

Detective Williams and Captain Haddock spoke quietly to each other at Williams' desk as they cautiously watched Mark. He came out of the restroom and walked back into the Captains office.

A distraught Julie was standing next to the desk, her face soaked with tears. Wiping her running nose on her sleeve, she looked up at him.

"Mark, I'm so sorry!" she stepped towards him, arms outstretched to embrace him. But he backed away.

"It's alright, Julie," Mark briefly held up his hand.

"You had no way of knowing that Nick was involved in killing Allie. I realize that, and I'm not upset with you at all," he sounded very cold.

"Oh, thank God, because it's true. If I had any idea something like that was going on, I would've gone straight to the cops!" Julie said sincerely. "If I could've saved her or protected her in any way… I would have."

"Of course you would have," Mark said nonchalantly. "I just wanted you to know that."

Julie stood back, noticing his detached behavior.

"Oh, okay. Thank you for that," Julie said quietly.

She tried to swallow the seemingly large lump in her throat. She looked at him, a bit confused as to why he was so different towards her. But she couldn't blame him.

"Sorry to hear about Nick and Lucy, though. That couldn't have been an easy thing to overhear," Mark sat down in the seat that he had been sitting in before her arrival.

"I wonder how long that's been going on," Mark said casually.

She shook her head slightly and looked down at her green scarf...tugging at the frayed edges with her trembling fingers. "I don't know... I, I have no idea," she stuttered.

Julie sat down in the other chair, and suddenly felt ... wounded. She turned her head and looked out the window.

Captain Haddock and Detective Williams came in then and began talking about the next steps of the investigation. The Police Department would continue investigating the possible poisoning of Allie, in which they now suspected Nick Butler. Julie signed her statement, and in doing so, agreed to testify against her estranged husband. She also agreed to wear a wire when she went home that night to retrieve her things. Any evidence to prove the affair between Nick and Lucy would only strengthen the connection in the pending murder charge. That would help the prosecuting attorney to prove some sort of motive. Also, it would be especially compelling evidence, in bringing in Lucy for the conspiracy charge.

"Nick was obviously carrying out Lucy's wishes. That was

very apparent from the conversation I overheard," Julie said. She was trying hard to think of any other clue she may have missed.

Mark glared at her and said, "What, are you the good wife all of the sudden, defending him now?" he said harshly.

Julie looked at Mark. "No! Of course not, Mark, I'm just telling you what I heard. Please, don't twist it that way," she stared back; mortified that he would even think that.

Haddock cleared his throat.

"I'm wondering who else is behind this. We need to start thinking about whom the other person might be that Lucy mentioned to Nick. You know, "The One" that's supposed to be arriving tomorrow and squaring up Nick," Williams contemplated.

"Yeah, if only there were someone like, OH, say... A CONVICTED MURDERER, that we could point the finger at! That would narrow things down considerably, don't you think?" Mark said sarcastically. "In fact, it would almost solve the case."

Haddock wasn't impressed. "I understand your suspicions, Mark. And they're very believable and compelling. But right now, Vanzetti's still in prison. We still don't know what will happen at his appeal tomorrow. Until then, we need to be able to consider other possible suspects. There's only one other person that we know, FOR SURE, that's coming into town. And that's Dom Angelo," Haddock stated.

Mark hadn't even thought about him. It was hard to suspect Dom of being capable of such betrayal. Something like this wouldn't be happening without him knowing about it, though. "Could it be?" Mark thought.

"I know that he's out of town right now, taking care of his sister, Anita," Mark said. "And he IS supposed to be here tomorrow for Allies autopsy…" Mark trailed off.

"But, according to Julie," Mark said rudely, "Lucy clearly said, 'Just wait one more day…HE would be there…and Nick would be rewarded,' " Mark quoted.

"Right, we're going to assume that that means a payment of some kind. Maybe it's a cash exchange, a payment for a job well done. That would be something Dom might likely handle, since Nick DOES work for him already," Captain Haddock added.

Julie shook her head in disagreement.

"I don't know, something doesn't make sense about Dom…I don't really think he'd be okay with Nick and Lucy…carrying on, unless, he just doesn't know about that part yet," Julie shuddered. The very thought of Nick and Lucy being together made her skin crawl.

"Who knows if Dom is really a part of this? At this point, I just assume everyone is involved now. If you don't get Nick and Lucy to spill the beans on each other about who, where, when, why and how…. there's going to be a blood feud tomorrow," Mark said frankly.

This revelation shocked Williams. Julie sat stunned, staring at Mark.

"Are you implying that you, yourself are going to handle this in your own way, if we don't produce the results you want, when you want them, Mr. Anderson?" Haddock asked seriously. "Are you threatening with bloodshed?"

Detective Williams and Julie silently watched and waited for Mark to answer.

"No. I am not implying that at all Captain Haddock. We're just dealing with a cold blooded killer here, whether you acknowledge it or not. Criminals, that might be looking to get rid of people who have become a liability. Why pay a scumbag you hired to do your dirty work, when you can just get rid of them afterwards. It's a money saver in the least," Mark said bluntly.

"I must have misunderstood you then, Mr. Anderson. I apologize for the confusion," Captain Haddock said awkwardly. "I see your logic. That's a very good point," he nodded.

"Well, I think we have a good idea of what's happening in the next 24 hours. Right now, let's just focus on tonight and hope we can get some good evidence from the wire," Williams said.

"Well, thank God we have a plan," Mark said sarcastically.

Julie felt that Mark was acting arrogant and was simply mocking the investigation. But she felt that she didn't have the right to judge him on how he should or shouldn't be acting. Despite her own feelings about it, she knew she shouldn't blame him for his temperament.

Detective Williams glanced at Julie, somehow knowing that

she was thinking the same thing he was.

Mark had always had a good moral compass, one that clearly defined that fine line between right and wrong, good and evil. It was getting harder to distinguish that faint line under the dim lights of his now harsh circumstances. Julie now understood that as a friend and someone who cared a great deal about what happened to him, she would now have to keep a close eye on Mark, just in case he was in need of someone to switch on a light for him when he could no longer see in the dark.

"We thank you again, Mrs. Butler, for your willingness to wear this wire tonight. It will be extremely helpful. If you don't mind going into the ladies room now with Detective Chavez, she'll be the one to get you all set up with that, okay, Mrs. Butler?" Captain Haddock said respectively.

"It's my pleasure, Captain Haddock. After tonight, sir, if you'll kindly refer to me as, "Ms. Allen," Julie almost smiled as she thought of how nice that sounded. She took one last glance at Mark, before she walked out of the room.

Mark sat motionless and stared blankly at the floor, pretending not to hear what Julie had just said. He didn't have time to care about her and Nick's marital issues, let alone her name status. He just wanted to get in that stake out van, and hear Nick's confession on that wire.

CHAPTER 11

WIRED

The Captain's instructions echoed in Julie's mind as she drove home that evening. She hoped she would remember everything. She tightened her grip on the steering wheel and focused on the road ahead of her.

"Don't instigate a fight or argue with him, just stick to the facts. You believe he has been cheating on you with Lucy, you need some time to think, and you're going to a hotel for a couple of days. Okay? Everything he says to you will be picked up by the wire. Detective Williams' will be listening in a nearby van that will be parked right around the corner. Other police officers and I are close by just in case. If anything should happen, we'll be there in ten seconds," Haddock said.

Julie took comfort in that last part. Her colleague at work said Nick hadn't been by, or called for her...so that meant she could pretend she was at work all day. Business as usual, it was time to go home. He might not even be there, she thought. He usually wasn't.

Julie pulled into the driveway and saw Nick's truck. Damn it.

She took a few deep breaths before getting out of the car and heading up to the house. Julie saw a faint glow of light on in the upstairs window. She paused for a moment and looked around at the outside of the house. For the first time in the seven years that they had lived there, she was frightened to go in. Everything looked completely normal and unchanged, yet everything felt so different. She had no idea what to expect and had even thought about just getting back in her car and driving away. But, instead, she gathered her strength and went inside. "We need answers for Allie," she told herself.

The houses warmth and the smell of vanilla candles comforted her. She had been burning those candles for Allie. She decided to just act as normal as possible and stick to her routine. Julie sauntered into the kitchen and tossed her purse on the counter.

Glancing in the sink, she absent mindedly looked for dirty dishes. It was one of the ways she could tell if Nick had eaten anything that day. Julie now realized just how pathetic this habit was. Hindsight could be so obviously cruel. Julie felt stupid, not acknowledging his drug use before. All the little signs now seemed like billboards framed in bright, Hollywood style, movie theater bulbs.

She heard Nick upstairs, blowing his nose in the bedroom.

She decided it was time to get this over with. Julie slowly walked up the stairs and crept into the hallway.

She could see him standing next to the bed, looking out the window as she peeked in through the crack in the door. She carefully and slowly pushed the door open.

Julie stepped into the room with her game face on. She looked annoyed, with her eyebrows slightly raised. It was almost a chore just to look at him. Nick turned and looked at her, he had obviously been crying.

"I know why you're here, and I know what your plan is," he said, staring at her. He jammed his hands in his pockets.

"You do?" Julie thought her heart might have just gone up into her throat. She thought for a second he might really know.

He looked away from her and squinted, like it physically hurt him, to look into her eyes.

"Before you go, just let me say a few things to you, please? Let me try to explain and then you never have to see me again!" Nick pleaded. He paced back and forth in front of the bed.

"Okay. Go ahead and say what you need to, Nick," Julie watched him cautiously.

"I know you're leaving me this time, and you're probably going to ask me to sign the damn papers, once and for all. That's fine. I don't blame you! I just want to say, that I'm sorry for the way this is ending. It's my fault... everything's my fault, entirely!"

He was weeping now. He wiped his nose on his sleeve.

"Holy hell, Jule's, you have NO idea. No idea at all!" He yelled.

Julie stood silently and listened to him. Trying to keep her heart from slamming outside her chest... she took long slow breathes to calm herself.

"Enlighten me. Give me an idea, so I know what's going on with you. I mean, I think you might owe me that much," she said cynically.

"I do owe you that," Nick acknowledged. "But you're not going to like what I have to say. I'm not the man that you thought you married. I never have been. I have always thought that I didn't deserve you, and now I know it's true. You're too good for me, Jules, and you always have been!" He snickered a little in between his sniveling. Julie stayed in front of the open door.

She cleared her throat. "So it's definitely true then, you and Lucy have been sleeping together? " Julie asked quietly.

"Yeah, it's true. What the heck," he looked down at the floor. "I might as well get it ALL out, right?" He smiled.

"How long have you been seeing each other?" Julie said louder. Trying not to raise her voice too much, but wanted it to be clear on the wire recording.

"Awhile, maybe a year or so, but you weren't supposed to find out. Definitely not like this anyway," he looked a little ashamed.

"Dom has been gone a lot taking care of his stupid sister and he's always busy with his 'Golden Boy' Mark… teaching him new shit! You were always at work or hanging out with 'Princess Allie', so what was I supposed to do, you know?" he laughed.

"Lucy gave me attention and made me feel like a man. I'll tell you what I ended up doing, though. I got myself mixed up in the wrong shit. That's what!" He sat down on the bed and put his head down into his hands.

"What do you mean? What kind of stuff did you get yourself mixed up in?" Julie tried not to sound too obvious, like she was coaxing him to say more.

"I've noticed you haven't been yourself …for quite some time. I knew we were drifting apart, but not like this," she said truthfully.

"We want different things in our lives, Jules. You want kids and a family life…with a picket fence and …I want to have fun! I want excitement in my life, to explore other… options."

He stood up and looked at Julie through red, watery eyes.

"I just don't want what you want. I never have. I just went along with it and it got to be too much to handle. So I got a little crazy, and a little ahead of myself. Now I don't know what I want or what the hell I'm doing anymore," Nick was swinging his arms, gesturing with his hands as he spoke.

"Are you on drugs?" Julie asked point blank.

"Why? What difference does that make?   We're not going to be together anymore…what difference does it make, Fuck! There you go again! What are you, my fucking MOTHER?" Nick suddenly became very defensive. She knew she had pushed a button.

"I'm sorry… you're right it doesn't matter. Not anymore, so… I'm going to get a few things and I'll be out of here. I'm going to stay in a hotel for a couple nights, and clear my head," Julie reached for the closet door, when Nick suddenly lunged forward and grabbed her by the wrist.

"Just let me finish saying what I have to say! Then you can pack your shit up. But right now, I'm trying to tell you something, Julie!! I'm trying to fucking talk to you!" Nick shouted in her face. She turned her head to the left.

"Let go of my wrist, Nick!" Julie yanked herself out of his grasp, and turned to face him.

"Don't you touch me, ever again," Julie's icy glare backed him off.

Julie wondered if the cops were on their way. Was Mark listening too? He wouldn't let anything happen to her, right?

"I'm sorry! I'm sorry…I just need to get this out…and then you can go! You don't ever have to see me again," Nick pleaded.

"Okay, then, finish!" Julie yelled back at him.

Nick walked back to the bed and sat down in the same spot where he had been sitting before.

"I did something bad, Jules. Something I thought was a good idea at the time," he shook his head back and forth.

Julie didn't say a word, she just kept listening. As Nick began to talk, he grabbed at the comforter he sat on, knotting it up in his hands.

"Lucy told me if I did this little favor for her, I could get all the dope I wanted and an easy... $500,000 cash. It sounded pretty good to me. I could take my money, my dope and Lucy...and move away from all this crap. Start a new life for ourselves," Nick daydreamed.

He was waving his hands above his head and looking up at them, like his future was on some magical map, and he was spreading it out on the ceiling.

"But it's not like that anymore! Shit's all messed up now!" He wiped his nose on his sleeve.

"It wasn't supposed to be her! It wasn't supposed to be her, Jule's! I swear!" Nick began hitting himself in the forehead with the palm of his hand, out of frustration.

"What are trying to say, Nick? It wasn't supposed to be who? Lucy?" Julie was shaking and felt sick to her stomach. The hair stood up on her arms as she anticipated his next words.

"NO! Not Lucy, Allie!" He blurted out.

"I'm the one who poisoned her. I killed her!" Nick was screaming it out now. His struggling conscience was being set free with every word he spoke.

"It was meant for Mark! The icing on his piece of cake that was served to him must have gotten mixed up, and put on Allies plate instead! Lucy hired a bunch of temporary workers from a place up town, so they wouldn't be suspicious or question anything."

"They sure as hell didn't know what we were trying to do! I'm telling you the truth. I didn't mean to kill her, I swear!" Nick yelled.

Julie was shaking uncontrollably. She couldn't believe what she was hearing. Nick fell onto the floor and crawled over to Julie, grabbing at her hands.

"Do you believe me, Jules? Please say you believe me! I didn't mean to kill that girl!" Nick was begging her to believe him.

"Yes. Yes, I do," she whispered in a raspy voice. Her salty tears flowed into the corners of her pursed mouth.

"I was just so sick and tired, of every little thing I worked so hard for, to just be HANDED on over to Mark on a silver fucking platter! All my time, all my hard work, that I put into that restaurant was all for nothing!" Nick stood and angrily stomped his foot.

"I decided I wasn't going to do it anymore. When was I supposed to get my big break? Where was my big promotion? I was tired of waiting. No one was just going to GIVE it to me! So, that's why I did, what I did! I wish I would've killed Mark instead," Nick felt like his actions were justified somehow.

Julie was devastated by what she heard come out of his mouth. He wasn't remorseful for the murder. He was upset that he hadn't killed the right person. He was a monster.

"Now, you know everything. So, you can go on and live your perfect life. I'm not going to fight you on anything, the house, the car, my truck, the money in our account...it's all yours. Okay? The divorce papers are signed. They're on the desk in the den," he smiled at her and nodded. He had said what he needed to and was satisfied.

Nick walked over to the bed and sat down again.

Julie nodded as the tears fell down her cheeks.

"I told Lucy, that you overheard us, and you called me out on it. So, I told her, as soon as this thing with you was over, we could take the money and go away together, just like we had planned. But, you know what she told me?" Nick asked.

"What?" Julie wept. "What did she say?"

"That the deal and our little arrangement we made, was off! She didn't think things were working out between us after all! She says I'll probably be implicated in the murder, and she'll be long gone by then. No more money for Nick, no nothing! She just used me," he was crying now.

"I have two choices, Jule's. I can either run or just end it all right now," he smirked.

Nick reached under the foot of the bed where he was sitting, and pulled out his 45 revolver.

"Oh, my dear, God!" Julie gasped and fell back into the closet door. "Put the gun away Nick...please?" she begged. "Please! We can go to the police, and we can tell them your side of the story. Nick, it doesn't have to be like this. It was an accident, right?" Julie pleaded with him.

Julie slowly straightened herself up and began to inch her way to the door. She saw shadows in the hallway moving along the staircase, out of the corner of her eye. She focused her blurry eyes on Nicks and made her way towards the door.

"The police? Are YOU on fucking drugs? Just get out of here Julie, go! Move on with your life! I just wanted you know that I'm sorry, and I didn't mean to kill Allie! So, GO!" Nick put the gun to his head.

She stood in the door way and whispered, "Once upon a time, I loved you. Good bye, Nick."

Julie's left arm was pulled abruptly, yanking her into the hallway. Someone had grabbed a hold of her and picked her up, cradling her in his strong arms. He now carried her swiftly down the stairs. She didn't have to guess who it was. She knew it was Mark.

The muffled sounds of the police rushed into the room and

their voices yelled, "Drop the gun, get down, and show us your hands!" The shouting echoed through the house. The blast of cold air on her face, made Julie open her eyes. She wasn't even aware that she had closed them. She saw a black SUV and realized that Mark was taking her there. He opened the door, helped her in and slammed the door shut.

CHAPTER 12

BAIT AND SWITCH

Julie was lying down in the back seat of the SUV. The cool leather felt good on her cheek. She lay there listening to all the commotion outside. She knew that they had Nick and were taking him to jail. She didn't want to look, for fear of laying eyes on him. She never wanted to see his face again. She thought she heard someone say something about having a search warrant.

This was all very surreal for her. Julie couldn't believe that this was all happening, even though she had watched it with her own eyes. She was hoping that for the most part, the worst of it was over. At least she hadn't watched Nick blow his head off.

Mark opened the door and stood there staring at her. He waited for her to sit up and move over, before getting in. He still hadn't said a word to her. She was going to say something to him, but before she could get a word out, Mark grabbed the front of her sweater wrap, jerked it open and began to unbutton her shirt.

Her eyes were wide with confusion. "Wha-What are you doing?" she stammered. Her heart pounded.

Mark slid his hand inside her unbuttoned shirt, grazing the soft skin above her belly button, and pulled on the microphone wire, releasing it from the clip that attached it to her bra. He held it up in front of her face so she would understand.

"Oh, yeah… thanks," she fumbled with fastening the buttons on her shirt and wrapped her sweater back around her, extra tight.

"I'll be right back. Don't get out unless I tell you to," Mark said sternly.

Julie had never seen him act so completely mechanical. She watched him give the wire to Captain Haddock, and then walk into the house.

Julie looked around at the neighborhood, buzzing with activity. Many people were trying to catch a glimpse of what was happening, standing in groups of three or more in their yards, gossiping. She didn't care what they thought in the slightest. She didn't like this neighborhood anyway.

Captain Haddock suddenly knocked on the window, startling her. He opened the door.

"Hello there, Ms. Butler," he smiled and nodded politely. "I mean, Miss Allen. We're going to leave your vehicle here for now, okay? We're taking you to a hotel tonight, where there will be officers patrolling the area, checking in with you and keeping an eye on your house. You will be perfectly safe, but we need you to call in to work for a couple of days, alright?" he said.

"Oh, that actually won't be necessary. I have the next couple of days off anyway. Will it be any longer than that?" Julie asked.

"We'll see. After the next couple of days, we'll hopefully know more, and then be able to make a decision on what's best for you at that time," he smiled impatiently.

He gestured toward the police car that was parked in the driveway.

"Is this like, local witness protection?" she asked.

"Yeah, kind of like that," he nodded.

"I need to wait for Mark, he said he'd be right back," Julie was looking over his shoulder trying to spot him, but he wasn't there.

"He'll be right along, Miss Allen. He's speaking with Detective Williams at the moment."

"I know, he just told me not to go anyplace unless he was here," Julie felt rushed.

Julie was staying in that SUV. She wasn't going anywhere without Mark's say so.

"It's okay, I assure you. Let's just get you in that car over there. I'll help you out," Captain Haddock held the car door open all the way now, and took a step back.

Julie began to panic. "Why is he making me leave without Mark? Mark said not to get out of the car" she thought. She didn't know who to trust anymore, and the stress was starting to get to her. She was more than a little cautious at this point, she was flat out paranoid!

"Look, Cpt. Haddock! Mark told me not to get out unless HE told me too. I hope you understand…but I have had a HELL of a day, and I'm waiting for the ONE person that I know I can trust right now. Do you understand that? Is that OKAY with you?" Julie reached out and grabbed the door, slamming it in the Captains face.

Captain Haddock backed away raising the palms of his hands, showing he had no problem with that, whatsoever.

"Uncle," he said as he turned around and headed back into the house, shaking his head.

Mark was in Julie's bedroom gathering a few things for her and putting them in a bag. He planned on taking her to the hotel where she would be hiding out for a couple days. Soon, the detectives would be picking up Lucy for questioning.

"If they can find her," Mark thought.

All signs seemed to be pointing at something happening the following day. Mark didn't want to take any chances with Julie's safety, so he would be the only one knowing where he was actually taking her. He went back downstairs to look for anything else he thought she might need.

Grabbing Julie's purse from the kitchen counter, Mark overheard Captain Haddock speaking to Williams on the front stoop.

"She's not getting out unless Mark is right there, so good luck getting her to budge," Captain Haddock was rubbing his temples out of exhaustion, glancing back at the SUV.

"Awe, don't take it too personally, Captain. She HAS been through a lot. I can't blame her for being on edge. So, if Mark told her to wait for him, then she's not going to go anywhere unless Mark HIMSELF escorts her," Williams said.

Mark smiled to himself and walked over to them to say goodbye.

"Thanks for all your help tonight, guys," Mark shook their hands. "We'll talk first thing in the morning, and uh… text or call me if there's any new developments between now and then," he looked at Williams.

"I'll be taking Julie to the Hotel, and getting her settled in the room," he stated. "I've been briefed on the room number."

Captain Haddock nodded. "Good night, Mark."

Mark took the keys out of Julie's purse and went out to start her car. He put the bag of her things in the back seat, and went to get Julie. Dusk was setting in.

When Mark opened the door, he noticed how frazzled she really was. She looked at him like a deer caught in the headlights. "Come on, let's go," he helped her out.

"Captain Haddock wanted me to go get in that other car, but you said not to," she was watching the police come out with bags of evidence. She nervously glanced at everyone.

"It's alright. I just didn't want you walking around, getting in the way or taking off, all vigilante style, like you did at the restaurant."

Mark, still stone faced, helped her into the car.

"Oh," she looked puzzled. "I guess... I was just a little jumpy, and maybe a little paranoid. I told him I had had one hell of a day. I hope he excuses my snapping at him."

Julie knew she was rambling, but didn't care. "I just want to get somewhere I feel safe and relax, you know? Like, take a nice hot shower and go to bed. Not that I would be able to sleep...but it's the thought that counts right?" she laughed nervously.

Mark tried not to look at her. "Being careful or cautious isn't the same as being paranoid. But, don't worry about it. You did fine," he said.

"I swapped your hotel for another one that they don't know about. They had you all set up and I made a last minute change to the reservation. Maybe I'm a little paranoid, too, but at least I'll know your safe," he focused on the road.

"Thanks for looking out for me," Julie said, searching his stoic face for a human reaction. But there was nothing. She didn't even know what to say to him to make small talk. It seemed weird and awkward. "I appreciate it," she said.

No... "You're welcome", or "No problem"... That would have been a good response, she thought.

She had never known until now, that stress and grief like what he's experienced lately, could actually change the way a person's face looked. He looked so uncaring, unfeeling. His eyes were hardened and dark. She had never imagined that he would ever look like this.

She also wondered if he blamed her for any of this. That's what bothered her the most. But he had heard Nick's confession, hadn't he? He had to know that she didn't have anything to do with this, let alone betray his friendship in any way.

What she didn't understand, if he knew all of this, why was he so cold and distant towards her? They were still friends, weren't they? But everything has changed now, she could tell. Maybe it was all too weird for him, to be friends with the wife of the man who killed his daughter, whether Nick had meant to do it or not. Who knows?

Was Nick telling the truth? Maybe he really WAS trying to kill Mark. She felt suddenly empty when she thought of that…of not having Mark in her life at all. As a friend or not, the idea of not having him there… was scary. What if Nick had succeeded? A sudden panic seized her stomach and knotted up in her gut. She couldn't even fathom the possibility. Her deep thought was interrupted by the car jerking to a stop in a The Comfort Plus parking lot.

"I'm going to walk up there with you and get you settled. No one knows what hotel or what room you'll really be staying in. I used an alias to book your reservation. It's under Mrs. Kadi Brown. Okay, Kadi?" Mark grabbed the bag that he had brought for her. "This is for you," he shoved it towards her.

"Oh, thank you," she said quickly.

She got out and tried to keep up with Marks pace. "Thanks for packing my things, and for the room…thanks for everything you've done for me," Julie stuttered as they speed walked down the quiet hallway trying to find the room number. Mark stopped.

"Try your key," Mark handed her the room key and stepped aside.

She swiped it and opened the door. Mark put his arm across her when she tried to go in. "What?" Julie asked.

"Hold on a second," he whispered sternly. He drew his gun from the left side of his jacket.

Mark flicked on the table lamp and glanced around the little room, waving her in.

She walked into the darkened room, dropped her purse and fell on her back, onto the bed.

Mark walked over to the window and moved the curtain, letting in a stream of moon light.

"Everything's fine Mark, don't worry," she rubbed her eyes.

"Don't worry?" Mark repeated her.

"Is he searching the bathroom?" Julie thought to herself.

"You said it yourself. No one knows I'm here, but you," she said lazily.

"Nick told Lucy that you overheard them talking in the office. Don't you get it? You're now a target. But you think you're safe and you can just relax now, right? Seriously, what do you think is going on here? Some sort of High school bullshit? He said, she said?" he asked sarcastically. Mark put his gun away.

Julie sat up from the bed and propped herself up onto her elbows.

"Umm... I don't really know, Mark! Why don't you tell me what's going on? It's a messed up situation. But excuse me, if I don't have the mental capacity for all of this shit like you do! Oh, and for the record, you're handling it like a PRO!" Julie shot him a dirty look and gave him a "thumbs up".

Mark glared at her. "You have NO idea what kind of people we are dealing with here! They're killers, who have tracked me down and managed to infiltrate my life for YEARS, just to get to me and revenge Lucy's piece of shit brother."

Mark was fuming. He hated that she acted so clueless.

"Lucy is Leo's sister?" Julie was surprised. "I had no idea."

"There's a lot going on here that you have no idea about. No one is safe, and that's why I'm taking a little extra precaution with you. If they think you mean something to me, they will try to hurt you, or kill you. They've already gotten to my daughter, what makes you think you're so special?" Mark's dark, icy glare burned into her.

Julie had reached her boiling point, and whether he deserved it or not… she was about to blow up on him.

"You know, you're right. Your completely right, Mark! What the hell makes me so damn special, huh?" Her eyes flashed with hurt and anger. She felt her face and ears grow hotter. She stood up and faced him now. She didn't care if her face was red and she was shaking like a leaf.

"Why are you even here? Why are you packing my bags and acting like my personal body guard, when you can't stand to be around me? Yet, I'm supposed to sympathize with your bad attitude. This hasn't exactly been a vacation for me either, you know! My friend's daughter dies, at her birthday party of all days, a young girl that I LOVE dearly and thought of as my OWN! Then I find out, my "friend" has this crazy secret life, and that we're all in danger!" Her breathing was short and gasping.

Julie began to frantically pace the floor. "To top it all off…I find out my estranged husband has been sleeping with another woman for damn near close to a year, and dumps me like yesterday's garbage… oh and let's not forget, that before he attempts to blow his head off in our bedroom…he tells me that he's the one that killed Allie!" Julie yelled.

She threw her hands up in the air, like two white flags surrendering… to GOD.

Mark stood at the door with his hand on the knob looking at her, his face still emotionless.

"So, yeah…thanks to you, I now know how completely UN special I am!" she stated.

"YOU, the only friend I can trust right now, acts like I'm a damn stranger, and won't even look at me or talk to me unless you're ordering me around or you absolutely have to! Don't get me wrong…I completely sympathize with your entire state of mind, but damn it, Mark! Why do you have to blame me?" Julie cried.

"What? I never said anything like that. I don't blame you for any of this," he stared intensely at her.

"I know that you do, Mark. I know that you blame me, on some weird level… for all of this.   Ever since you found out about Nick's involvement, you've been nothing but distant and cold. I know that our "friendship" has taken a huge blow. I can feel it," she tapped her chest hard, directly over her heart.

"I don't blame you for what Nick has done. Just get that idea out of your head," Mark said quieter.

"Look, I do care about you Jule's, you have to know that by now, very much. But now is not the time to discuss our feelings! Given everything that has happened, to both of us… neither one of us can trust how we might or might not feel. We're grieving on all levels, and now is not the time to try to figure this out," Mark turned the handle and opened the door to leave.

Julie spoke softer. "I know that you feel like you can't trust anyone, and I totally get it. But if there's anyone in this world that you can be sure of… it's me," her voice cracked.

Mark stopped in the door way and turned around to face her. His dark, hard stare focused on her, searching her eyes for a sign of validity.

Julie had never in her life, felt more vulnerable than she did right then. Her eyes began to tear up and her bottom lip quivered as she felt her tough exterior softening.

Mark's eyes burned into hers, as he stepped back into the room, and shut the door behind him.

CHAPTER 13

LETTING GO

Mark rushed at her with such fierceness, that it stopped the breath in Julie's throat. He reached out and grabbed the back of her neck, passionately kissing her firmly on her lips. His kiss deepened as she opened her mouth to kiss him back.

His lips were incredibly soft and his tongue was electric. Instant heat radiated through her body, melting away all her defenses. She has wanted him secretly for so long now, that it felt natural and only right to finally be in his arms.

Julie's hands flew up and grabbed a handful of his thick, dark hair. She knew now, that he wanted to be with her just as much.

Julie began to peel back his leather jacket, off of his wide, muscular shoulders. She yanked down hard, hearing it thud as it hit the floor. His body pushed against her, backing her up to the bed. Breaking off the kiss for a moment, he took off his guns and set them safely on the floor. He quickly took off his shirt in one swift movement. Whatever emotional barriers he had that held him back before, were definitely gone now. All of the repressed anguish and sorrow that he felt was now being transformed into his insatiable need for her.

He ripped her sweater open and tossed it to the side. Mark grabbed a section of her buttoned blouse with his hands and yanked it open, not fumbling with them this time as the buttons scattered across the floor. Their hands were now intertwined in each other's hair as they kissed feverishly. Tugging her head back slightly, he ran his tongue down the side of her throat. He opened his mouth wide and pressed it to her neck, biting down on her. The mixture of wet heat and teeth sent shivers down her spine, and spread across her entire body.

Mark ran his hands down the front of her breasts, to her waist. He felt around for the top of her pants and unbuttoned them, sending them down her legs to the awaiting floor.

Mark hooked his fingers under the straps of her bra and gently pulled them down her shoulders, reaching around with one hand, he unhooked it, sending that to the floor as well. He stood up straight, breaking the spell of their long, magnetic kiss.

Looking down at her face in the moonlight, he tenderly held the back of her head as he held her close. He paused to watch her breasts rise and fall with each breath she took. Julie's body shook with anticipation.

"I have wanted you for so long… I just told myself it would never happen," he whispered.

That's when Julie saw it… that warmth, that softness in those gorgeous, hazel eyes that melted her every time. That look that she had come to love so much.

His tender expression changed to concern. "This is going to change everything, Jules. We shouldn't go any further unless it's what you really want."

Julie reached up and gently traced the outline of his thick, perfect eyebrows with her thumb. "Feels like velvet," she thought.

"Everything has already changed," she said quietly. "I've always wanted you, from the moment I first saw you and I know that I always will... regardless, of your name."

CLICK.

Mark reached down and grabbed her thighs, effortlessly lifting her up to his waist. Julie tightly wrapped her legs around him, throwing her arms around his neck and kissing him fervently. He turned his body and carried her towards the large window, putting her back against the wall.

Julie felt him lift her higher to adjust himself. She gripped him with her thighs to hang on tighter. Mark reached in between their bodies, carefully sliding his fingers inside the crotch of her panties, pulling them off to one side.

The feel of his strong hand brushing gently against the inside of her thigh and his fingers lightly touching her, sent a shocking sensation straight to her core. Julie let out a moan, as her left arm flung out to the side. Her hand eagerly searched for something to grab hold of, but felt nothing but the flat cool wall.

"Just hold on to ME," Marks raspy voice simmered into her ear, as Julie's body surrendered to his, trusting him completely.

~

Julie drowsily awoke to the smell of brewed coffee. All she could remember was being with Mark.

"Typical girl," she thought. Julie slowly realized where she was. She opened her eyes as the harsh reality set in. The reality being that... Allie was still dead. Nick was a suicidal murderer and people might be trying to kill her too. She wished it were all just a really bad dream.

Rubbing her eyes and brushing the unruly, still damp hair from her face, she sat up. The only light was coming from a single lamp on the kitchenette table. Glancing towards the window, she saw that the sun was coming up. Julie opened the curtains to let in the golden light.

"Mark?" she asked aloud. No response.

She noticed the bag he had packed for her, laying in the chair and got up to sort through it. Julie quickly got dressed into a comfortable pair of jeans and a long sleeve shirt before sitting down at the table to brush out her hair. She noticed Marks cell phone lying on the table there.

Quietly putting down her brush and looking around to assure herself that she was in fact the only one in the room, she opened up his phone to take a quick peek. Keeping the fact that, Mark, wouldn't have gone too far without it in the back of her mind. She was just a little curious.

Suddenly, the phone received a text message. Startling her

with its vibration, she yelped and put the phone down. Glancing around and realizing once again that she was indeed alone; she opened it to read the text.

It was from Detective Williams. "Got our warrant and picked her up at 7:00 a.m."

"Oh, thank goodness!" Julie thought.

Julie heard the hotel key slide through the lock. She turned with the phone in her hand just as Mark came in. He had a paper bag in one hand and a magazine rolled up with today's paper in the other.

"Well, good morning," he greeted her with a smile. "Did you have fun snooping through my phone while I was out getting your breakfast?"

"I'm sorry, you got a text from Detective Williams," she handed it out to him and sat down at the table again.

Mark sat down across from her and placed the bag between them. Julie smelled sausage and eggs. He quickly read it and closed his phone with a snap, sliding it inside his inner jacket pocket.

"I'm going to have to leave soon… I have a busy day ahead. I need to stop by the precinct to hear about Leo's parole hearing as well," Mark said.

He got up and poured two cups of the brewed coffee. He sat down putting one in front of Julie.

Julie sat quietly and smiled as she watched Mark lay down a napkin and put a breakfast sandwich and a little hash brown in front of her.

"Thank you... that looks great," she smiled at him. "It was very nice of you to get me food."

His sweetness was almost amusing to her. She loved that about him. He was always so kind... so courteous.

"You're very welcome. You worked up quite the appetite. I bet your starving," his eyes smoldered into hers as he took a sip of his coffee. That grin would be the death of her.

Julie blushed, remembering last night. They had made love and stayed up till the early morning hours talking... before they made love again. The heat began to rise, as she remembered.

She cleared her throat, refocusing her thoughts on the day's events.

"As you know... I'm not going to work today and I could be ready in just a second and come with you if you want," she mentioned.

Mark appeared hesitant.

"I really need you to stay here, Jules. It's not that I don't want you with me... It's just that I want you to be safe and stay as far away from things as possible," he replied.

"I understand," she took a drink of her coffee and tried not to seem so disappointed.

"This has nothing to do with last night, absolutely nothing to do with us…. so don't think for a second that I'm doing the typical man thing and blowing you off. So… don't do the typical woman thing and sit there and pout," Mark said jokingly.

Julie smiled. "No. I really do understand. Captain Haddock told me that I need to stay here. I have a confession to make though… I read your text. So I know you're curious about what's going on with Lucy. So am I," Julie began to eat her breakfast.

"I figured as much," he smiled. "I don't mind that you read my text, at all."

"I'm not sure what's going to happen today, or how things are going to unfold…but I would feel a hell of a lot better knowing you were here. I need to know that you're alright, even if you're bored," he said with a half-smile.

"Which reminds me, I picked up a newspaper and a magazine for you!" He quickly flipped through the pages of the magazine lying on the table.

"You also have room service, cable and that awesome jetted tub," he mentioned.

She blushed… again.

"Before you know it, the day will be over. What more could you ask for? Besides me, of course," he flashed his famous grin.

His playful expression changed as he looked at is watch.

"What time is it, anyway?" Julie asked in between bites.

"It's a quarter to eight. I should probably be heading out now," he said seriously.

Mark looked at her for a long moment. "Thank you for last night. I feel like I'm the luckiest man alive to have shared this time with you. You're such a wonderfully loving and passionate woman. Next to my mother, you're the kindest person I have ever known. Last night meant more to me than you will ever know," his expression was somber as he reached over and took her hand.

"It meant a lot to me too, Mark," Julie said cautiosly.

Julie's forehead wrinkled in confusion. She leaned over the table to look into his face. "Why are you talking to me like you're never going to see me again?" Julie was worried now.

"I have this horrible feeling that you're going to do something stupid, and probably homicidal. So, DON'T," Julie squeezed his hands.

Mark clenched his jaw and looked away from her.

"Please, Mark, don't let those horrible people turn you into something you're not. I understand your NEED... to be a part of this investigation and I'm going to stay out of your way and let you handle things however you think you need to, but please don't take matters into your own hands. More people will end up hurt, or worse...killed. That includes you. Enough innocent people have died," Julie's eyes were pleading with him, searching his face for an indication of understanding.

Mark stood and walked around the table to Julie. He reached down and carefully brought her up to him and he hugged her and softly kissed her goodbye.

"I have unfinished business that needs taken care of... that's all. I promise you, that you will see these eyes again," his eyes twinkled when he smiled down at her. He cupped her face in his hands.

"I love you, Julie and I always will," he whispered.

"I love you too, and I always have," Julie replied with a smile.

~

As Mark walked away from the hotel, he focused his newly found energy on the task at hand. Leo wanted HIM right? Well, he would have his wish. Even if it meant sacrificing himself to end it all, he would. Mark knew that his legacy would live on through Julie and that her future would be safe and secure. By the end of this day, Leo, Lucy and Dom would pay for whatever their individual parts were in the injustice done to his family. If Mark was going to go down today, they were all going down with him.

CHAPTER 14

SLEEPING DOGS

Marks phone began to ring as he walked around the corner to the police station. It was Williams.

"Mark, I've got bad news. Lucy and her lawyer "walked" about thirty minutes ago. Without a confession or hard evidence, we were having a hell of a time finding something to hold her on but... that's not the only reason I'm calling. Where are you anyway? You're not at your house or the hotel," Williams said frantically. He must have been driving around looking for Mark.

"I'm at the police station now, apparently a half hour too late," Mark replied as he walked up to the precinct. "I had some things to take care of this morning. But I'm here now."

"Alright, I'll meet you in Haddock's office then," Williams hung up.

~

"Good morning, Mr. Anderson," Captain Haddock shook Marks hand and smiled.

"Please come in, we've had some developments this morning that I would like to discuss with you," Haddock gestured towards his office.

Mark walked into the familiar room, and sat down in the same brown leather chair he sat in the day before. He glanced up at the clock and saw it was almost eleven o'clock.

"Good morning, Sir. Detective Williams just told me you had Lucy, but you had to let her go with her lawyer," Mark said calmly.

"Yes, we weren't able to get anything out of her though. Except, her opinions about Nick, and how he's so messed up on drugs, you can't believe a word he says. We started in on her about Leo and out came the magic word, "Lawyer". We couldn't arrest her for anything just yet, so we had to let her go. But now we think we know who the "Man" is that she's meeting up with today, the one that Julie may have overheard her talking about," Haddocks' expression was worrisome.

Haddock was concerned about what Mark might do, how he was going to react. But, there was no easy way to say it. There was no sense in putting off the inevitable.

"Now, this is pure speculation, but it's got a little weight to it. We think that the man she's meeting up with today is simply her husband, Dom Angelo. He was the first person she called. It was him who sent the lawyer. The tail we put on Lucy just reported that Dom has arrived at his home just a few minutes before you arrived here," Haddock glanced up at two officers now standing outside of the office door. They were all watching Mark very closely.

"Relax," Mark looked at them. "I'm cool. I won't be causing a scene today fellas."

Williams came walking in now, observing the officers awkwardness, and sat down next to Mark, looking at Haddock.

"What am I missing?" Williams asked.

"I have already suspected that Dom could be involved, so this isn't a surprise to me at all," Mark continued the conversation.

"Well, forgive me for anticipating your reaction. You've been through your share of surprises over the last few days and no one would blame you if you were upset." Haddock said reasonably. "We just don't want you entertaining any notions of confronting them on your own. That would be a big mistake," Haddock said sympathetically.

Mark nodded in agreement.

"Honestly… the way I see it is, there's nothing I can do at this point, but to accept the truth, whatever it may be and allow justice to take it's natural course. Anything I do at this point could be detrimental to the case… and that would definitely delay any progress that we've made so far," Mark said simply.

Mark looked steadily at Captain Haddock. "One careless stride in the wrong direction, could wipe out the entire case. I'm not willing to jeopardize it," Mark said with conviction.

Williams leaned back in his chair and watched Mark now; with his eyes half squinting… he didn't believe what he was hearing. But then he quickly looked away, not wanting to give away his real thoughts on the matter.

Captain Haddock was awestruck. He seemed to think that Marks suddenly calm disposition was out of exhaustion. "This poor man has been drained, he's got no "fight" left in him," he thought.

Mark sat in the musty office watching Captain Haddock and Detective Williams talk back and forth, not listening to a word spoken. Williams glanced at Mark periodically for approval on the plans that Mark had absolutely no interest in. Mark would nod, pretending to comply.

His calm composure and relaxed nature never wavered for a second.

"Have you heard anything about Leo's board hearing?" Mark asked unexpectedly.

Haddock looked at Williams who stiffened up in his chair and shot him a look that all but said, "Don't say a word."

Haddock shrugged it away and said "It's alright Williams. I think he can handle it."

Mark saw this exchange and said, "I'm assuming that means he was paroled. Was he released already?" Mark asked bluntly.

"The hearing was about an hour and forty five minutes ago, and you're correct in assuming. It was granted based on his impeccable prison record and the positive work towards his rehabilitation. The board was quite impressed with his positive attitude," Haddock answered.

Williams grimaced.

"I find it hard to believe that such a cold blooded killer has been rehabilitated the way he has on paper, and received such honorable merit over the last thirteen years. But, according to these transcripts they sent over, he's the model prisoner."

Williams picked up a file and threw it back down, un-enthused by its contents.

Haddock continued to explain.

"We notified the warden and voiced our concerns. There wasn't much we could say or do to sway their opinions without evidence linking him to anything. Without a confession from Lucy, or more information from Nick, it's all circumstantial at this point. Our hands are tied."

Haddock sat back in his Captains chair and crossed his arms.

"I'm fairly confident that he won't be a problem. He has no money or means for transportation, let alone access to a plane ticket, they'll be watching him like a hawk. He had to check in immediately after his release anyway, with his parole officer. He's checked into the halfway house and everything. So it's got to be Dom that Lucy spoke of," Haddock speculated.

"Please tell me, that you're not denying Leo's connection, Captain. They'll all be meeting up soon, who knows, they more than likely have a plan to get him over here," Williams added.

"I'm not denying anything Detective, nor am I fabricating

conclusions. I'm simply explaining the process in which this investigation will be handled," Haddock seemed disgruntled by William's attitude.

"You will, still be tailing Dom and Lucy, right?" Mark asked.

"Yes! Except… we may have already lost Dom," Haddock looked disappointed.

"What?" Williams leaned forward and put his hands on his knees.

Mark's heart skipped a beat as he focused on Haddock, waiting for an answer, maintaining his composure.

"I was going to tell you after our conversation with Mark, but since his temper has diminished, I can probably tell you both. Dom's car was followed to the foothills and was lost by our officers that were tailing him," Haddock's brow furrowed. "It's only a momentary set back and we'll find him soon enough."

"Okay, was Lucy with him? Do they know who all was in the vehicle?" Williams was beside himself.

"As far as they know, it was just Dom and his driver. Lucy is still in their home. He wasn't there but a few minutes before he was seen leaving again. The reality of this situation with Dom is we have nothing on him. We couldn't even bring him in for questioning. He'd be out quicker than Lucy," Haddock looked at Mark, who was looking at him patiently.

"I'm sorry, Mark. Right now we need to focus on Lucy and Nick, and not so much on Leo and Dom. Nick is being held in the hospital in a psychiatric ward for a seventy two hour hold. He's under a twenty four hour surveillance camera. It's a mandatory hold for suicidal patients. Then he'll be transferred to county and be placed in solitary confinement. Until then, we just have to wait and see what transpires," Haddock was trying to be optimistic.

"At least we got her killer. The rest will follow suit, eventually. Don't worry, we'll keep a close watch on Julie's hotel room and notify you of any developments," Haddock seemed very pleased with himself.

"Believe you me... I understand the politics of an investigation and know how hairy things can get, don't worry about it. Thank you for all your hard work," Mark said sincerely.

Knowing that Julie was safe and that they didn't have a clue which hotel she was actually in, let alone which room, made him feel more confident. Mark had also moved her car that morning to another location... he just wanted to be extra cautious.

Haddock looked down at his desk.

"I also understand that your daughter's autopsy is being performed sometime this week, possibly today. I'm sorry. I'm sure that this isn't an easy day for you in the least. Just one more thing for you to think about, but, at least you'll have a scientific and medical cause of death. I hope that in the long run, it gives you some peace, and perhaps a little closure."

Mark held his body still and kept his movements fluid, as he fought to stay calm. It mentally derailed and disturbed him, thinking of her body as being dissected for an official, medically accepted cause of death. He thought of something else to dissuade his morbid thoughts.

"Thank you, Sir. I appreciate your kind words. You know, I just thought of something… you might try to find Dom at the hospital. He told me that he's going to talk to the doctor today about Allies autopsy and take care of everything as far as the arrangements go. He'll be there signing all the necessary papers, I'm sure of it," Mark said calmly.

Haddock sprang into action. He immediately called in the two officers he had posted outside his door and told them to head to the hospital. Williams watched Mark skeptically.

"Let's go get some lunch; you look like you haven't eaten in days," Williams stood and gestured toward the door.

Mark grinned and said, "Sounds like a plan to me. Let's let these officers get back to work, shall we?"

CHAPTER 15

GOD SPEED

"So are you going to tell me what your plan is, or do I have to figure it out?" Williams said frankly.

Mark sat comfortably in the passenger seat of William's car looking out the window at the passing trees.

"What do you mean? I don't have a PLAN... I'm just sitting back now and letting the police handle it from here on out," Mark said believably.

Unfortunately, Detective Williams didn't believe that for a second. He was getting pretty annoyed at Marks casual attitude

"Bullshit, Mark, you totally just sent them on a wild goose chase to the damn hospital... I could see that clear as day!" Williams was losing his patience.

"What ... is Dom performing the damn autopsy himself? NO, handling paperwork? NOT likely! He has people that do errands and things like that for him. He's not going to be there doing paperwork or making any phone calls. You and I both know he's not there doing anything. Just because he might be paying for it all doesn't mean jack! He's probably busy getting Vanzetti here, as-we-speak!"

Williams took a deep breath and focused on the noon traffic.

"Whoa! I'm impressed, Williams! I didn't realize you could be so passionate!" Mark laughed.

"Mark!" Williams snapped his fingers. "Earth to Mark… I'm serious. When are you going to start trusting me? You and I both know that Lucy can't do all this on her own… and Dom is the only one that's capable of putting something like this in motion. He has the means to get Vanzetti here if he wanted too. We need to collaborate and figure out where and when they're meeting up. They're not stupid."

Williams couldn't have been more serious.

Mark spoke very nonchalantly.

"I don't know. I doubt that anything's going to go down today. I mean, after Nick's mental breakdown, he was spewing confessions… and Lucy being brought in for questioning… you know that they're laying low. Like you said, they're not stupid. There's too much heat on them right now. The cops and all those detectives on this case got this one… it's just a matter of time, that's all. Some things you just can't rush," Mark was chewing on his lip, looking out the window.

Williams looked at Mark like he had just said the alphabet backwards and in another language.

"WHAT? No… You know what? I took a leap of faith,

trusted you and believed in you when I had every reason NOT to!"
Williams glared in Marks direction.

"There was something about your story that told me that I
needed to help you find out what really happened to your daughter.
It sounded so insane, that it had to be true. And I thought all you
really needed was someone to listen to your version. You had no
one to trust... and there I was. And here I AM, still! So please, let
me help you finish this. If I'm anything to you at all, I'm your
friend, Mark!"

William's looked straight forward with his hands on the
wheel and abruptly parked the car in a diner parking lot.

"Then you also remember the part about "walking away"
when it turned dangerous. It's about that time, Detective," Mark
said seriously.

"Think of your own daughter... and the career you've built
for yourself. Is it worth it to you, to lose it all over my personal
problems?" Mark unbuckled his seat belt and rested his hand on
the door handle. "I have nothing. No family, no career, zero, to live
for. I'm not going to let anyone else die for me," Mark spoke
calmly.

Detective Williams listened to Mark, alarmed by what he
was saying.

"What I need to do now doesn't have anything to do with
you. So I don't require your services any longer as a hired
investigator, but as a friend, I would humbly ask for your silence.
Please, go back to the precinct and tell Haddock you talked me into

going home to rest after lunch, and you'll notify me of any changes that take place regarding the case," Mark took out an envelope from the inside pocket of his leather jacket, handing it over to Williams.

"This should more than cover your fee, for helping me," Mark was trying to be professional. He needed this to be a business transaction, and nothing more.

"I don't want your money, Mark, you're not thinking straight. You're going to get yourself killed and then what good would that do, huh? What about Julie... I know you care about each other. It's obvious. Don't do anything you might regret," Williams pleaded.

"Julie is safe... I've made sure of that," Mark replied calmly.

Williams leaned back into the driver's seat, realizing the gravity of the situation.

"Yeah, I know. I had a feeling you were going to switch hotels when you insisted on taking her. You must have paid the desk clerk at the old hotel really well... because she told the reporting officers this morning that Julie not only arrived, but is still in her room!" Williams smiled, impressed by Marks cleverness.

"Which reminds me," Williams said.

He turned his body to face off with Mark. "I texted you this morning, at 7:30 a.m., and told you we had Lucy. I thought you'd be at the station with bells on. Instead, you shut your phone off and disappeared until about 11:00. That's when I was finally able to get a hold of you. Where were you?" Williams looked at Mark with skepticism.

Mark smiled. "A real gentleman doesn't kiss and tell," he insinuated.

"Oh. Say no more," Williams chuckled.

"Alright, man. I've got to go," Mark held out his hand to Williams and he shook it firmly.

"Thank you for everything. I know you'll keep at this investigation until everyone involved in my family's murders are brought to justice. You're a good man and a loyal friend. If there's anything about this crazy scenario worth believing, I believe in that," Mark patted his shoulder.

Williams knew that this might be the last time he saw him. He had no idea what Mark's plan was. It could be anything or nothing at all. Maybe he would just disappear completely off the face of the earth this time. He hoped he would get Julie and move away from all of these bad memories. Start anew. Heck… he didn't have the slightest idea.

"Good luck, my friend, God speed," Williams said.

Mark quickly got out of the car. He pulled the hood from his sweatshirt he wore under his jacket, up and over his head. It had started to rain. Williams watched as he walked behind an old brick building, and disappeared.

~

Detective Williams walked into the precinct like he had any other day. He sauntered up to Haddocks office and knocked on the door. Haddock looked up from his turkey sandwich and potato chips he had spread out on the desk. He waved Williams in.

"I'm sorry to interrupt your lunch, Sir. I just wanted to ease your mind about something," Williams leaned into the room.

"Oh, I could always use some good news, Williams. What's on your mind?" Haddock asked.

"Well, after a long talk with Mark over lunch, he's decided to go back to his house and get some sleep, poor guy. I told him that if anything came up, anything at all, I would text him or call him immediately," Williams said.

"Oh, that is good news! I mean, I have all the compassion in the world for that guy but, it's best that he take a break from all this. Let us handle things as we see fit," Haddock said, as he took a big bite of his sandwich.

"Yeah, well… I'm sure eating a meal for the first time in days helped out a little too," Williams smirked.

"I bet. It's got to be hard to go back to an empty home, where there's nothing but reminders of your daughter. Hell, I'd stay in a hotel room. No reminders there," Haddock mumbled.

Williams thought about what Haddock had just said. Detective Williams realized at that moment, that Mark had no intention of moving on with his life. There was no way that Mark would go back to that empty house and be able to continue.

"I'm fairly confident that Mr. Butler will be released from his evaluation and once he's of sound mind and in our custody, we'll be able to get some answers from him that we need to pick up Lucy. As for Mr. Vanzetti, he would have to be one smart son of a bitch to pull one over on the parole officers in fancy New York, City to even try to come here. Everyone seems to think something's going down today... but not with Leo Vanzetti. That man just got out of prison.   He wouldn't make it here today even if he wanted to," Haddock reasoned with himself.

"So, basically... you're focusing on pitting Nick and Lucy against each other or getting them to roll on Dom ... and then once you have sufficient evidence, then you'll pick up Vanzetti?" Williams was trying to get an idea of where the case was going.

"Yeah, sure. That's what I'm saying. I mean, if he is even involved and there really is a connection. I'm not real convinced of that just yet," Haddock said.

"Surely you see the connection between Vanzetti and his sister... given what Nick confessed to about Lucy... this definitely looks like a revenge killing that was obviously premeditated. We're talking conspiracy to commit MURDER here Captain," Williams tried not to show his frustration.

"We also can't base our questioning on the ranting's of a known drug addict, Detective. We need more proof to bring up charges of conspiracy to arrest Vanzetti. So far, all we have is circumstantial evidence. We have Julie's testimony that she "overheard" Lucy and Nick talking. She never actually saw Lucy; they could argue it wasn't even her. Nicks wiretap confession was a good idea, but that might not be admissible in court. There is a method to all of this. Just trust in the system. We're all giving this case the attention it deserves, but we do have other cases to work," Haddock said.

"Okay? That's the truth of the matter, and that's how we're going to be proceeding. I have a family of my own, Williams. I know this is a sensitive case. It always seems personal when a child is involved," Haddock said truthfully.

"Yes, Sir, I understand. Maybe taking a break today doesn't sound so bad, you know." Williams eased up and took a deep breath, blinking his eyes like it was going to clear out his mind. Williams leaned up against the newly made door frame.

"Then, take a break Williams. Go call your daughter or something... I'll let you know when Nick is transported from the hospital. I'm serious now," Haddock did look serious.

"I understand you're worried about things, but you're not going to miss anything. It's all out of our hands today. Let the pieces fall where they may, and THEN we might be able to put this puzzle together," Haddock's hands slapped down on the desk, emphasizing his point.

"Alright, then, I think I'll do that, Captain. I'll take the rest of the day off. Have a good day, Sir, thanks," Williams said.

"You too, Williams, it's not a problem! We've got to look

out for each other right?" Haddock said.

"We sure do, Sir," Williams smiled as he walked out of the Captains office.

~

William's quietly sat in his car and closed his eyes. He had so much on his mind, he just needed to take a step back and see it for what it was… without over processing it all. He had a tendency of over thinking things until it became warped into something it wasn't.

Mark was right about the precinct underestimating the situation. Captain Haddock was a good man and a good Captain, but his instincts were lacking and his actions were political. Williams issue with this was more than a professional disagreement, it was a moral dilemma. He knew in his gut that Leo was coming today and that Mark would be facing him alone. Dom and Lucy could have had this planned out for a long time… and nothing was going to stop it now. That was clear to him. If Captain Haddock couldn't see that too… then there was just no point in trying to change his mind. William's hands were also tied, and he has no choice but to follow the orders of his Captain. So, that's exactly what he'll do today.

Detective William's decided to take his first unscheduled day off, in almost six years. He was going to try to find Mark and help protect his partner and friend, from whatever mess he was about to get himself into. The first place he thought to look was Mark's house. Surely he wouldn't go back there… but maybe there was something there that could help lead him in the right direction.

Just as he began to pull out of the parking lot, William's cell phone rang. He pulled it out of his jacket pocket and glanced at it. "Who the heck is this calling me?" he wondered. The number didn't look familiar to him.

"Detective Williams," he answered.

"I'm sorry, this is who?" Williams was dumbfounded. He had heard who it was, the first time. He just couldn't believe his ears.

"Absolutely, where would you like to talk? I was just there, but YES! That's fine. I'll be there in about two minutes."

So much for the afternoon off, William's day just got a whole lot more complicated.

He hung up the phone and felt more confused and uncertain than he ever had.

"I'm seriously going to need a REAL vacation, after this is all over," Williams said aloud. He proceeded to turn his car around and head back into the precinct.

CHAPTER 16

UNFORESEEN

Using his work keys, Mark came in through the back door of the restaurant. Re-locking the door behind him, he punched the code into the security pad and reset the alarm. As he walked through the dining hall towards the vestibule, a piece of paper taped up on the inside of the glass, caught his eye. He hadn't noticed it there earlier, and decided to give it a closer look.

"We are temporarily closed, due to unforeseen personal circumstances. We are very sorry for any inconvenience this may have caused. Sincerely, Angelo's Management and Staff," Mark read aloud.

"Unforeseen?" He scoffed. What a joke.

Making his way back towards the kitchen, he began to check on the hidden cameras that he had secretly installed there earlier that morning. The one he had strategically placed in the lobby was still secure.

After leaving Julie at the hotel, Mark had stopped by his house and gathered the cameras from his own home security system. He thought that while Lucy was still in custody, and Dom was out of town, it would be the perfect window of opportunity to set his plan in motion.

Hanging a left, just through the silver double doors, he swiftly walked down the narrow hallway to Dom's office, unlocking the door. Mark looked to the top of the filing cabinet, knowing right where the camera was hidden. It was still there. Besides Dom, only Lucy and Mark had a key to that office. But, everything seemed untouched, and it appeared that nothing had been tampered with. He locked the door behind him and quietly walked back down the hall towards the kitchen. The last camera was mounted between a stack of bowls and a pile of old menus on a high shelf. It would span the entire kitchen, showing the dining room entrance.

Feeling confident that everything was where it should be and was going according to plan, he meandered into the dry storage room.

There, he stood up on a plastic bin and reached up towards the ceiling. He lifted up a ceiling tile and set it off to the side. Hoisting himself up into the dark musty opening, he carefully distributed his weight evenly on the structured steel frames. He carefully replaced the ceiling tile and situated himself into a semi comfortable position. Reaching out to feel with his left hand, he searched blindly, until he felt the canvas bag that he had also stashed that morning.

Feeling for the zipper, he grasped it and jerked it sideways. He felt inside, finding his flashlight. Mark clicked it on and held it in his mouth to free up his hands. Finding the remote control to the cameras, he put the bag down next to him.

According to the "D.I.Y Home Security System", he had approximately twelve hours of audio and visual recording time, upon pressing the remotes trigger button.

Marks plan was to get as much incriminating evidence as he possibly could recorded on both video and audio. He would confront them all and get them to talk... once he felt like he had enough evidence... he would make sure that Leo, Lucy, and Dom would pay for whatever part they each had in the murder of his daughter.

In the envelope with the money he gave to Williams, he disclosed Julie's location and that of her car. He had also left a note in Julie's car revealing the locations of the cameras and evidence he hoped to collect. He felt that he had entrusted the right people to take the evidence in and bring his plan of final legal justice to fruition.

The biggest gamble he felt, however, was the location of the meeting itself. Mark hoped "they" would figure that the restaurant was the safest, most private meeting place to get away from watchful eyes. His gut feeling told him that it would happen here anyway. After all, were they not Italians? Everything exciting always happens in the kitchen.

With his finger on the remote button, he waited patiently. God only knew how long he would be sitting there, but that didn't matter to Mark. It would all be worth it in the end.

~

It couldn't have been more than an hour when Mark heard the back door bang against the outer brick wall. He hated it when people swung it too hard. "Don't they realize that it can't possibly be good on the door?" he had always wondered. That could be Lucy, he assumed. She treated everything like it was expendable.

The scraping sound of high heels scuffed the concrete floor. This, followed by a series of beeps, told Mark that the alarm was disabled and it was indeed Lucy. She was apparently leaving the back door unlocked. Mark pressed the remote button and carefully set it down next to the flashlight on the bag.

"Go wait out in the car! As soon as my brother gets here, pay the cab driver and show him in!" Lucy snapped.

"Yes, Ms. Angelo," said a young males voice.

"That must be her driver," Mark thought. He heard him close the door behind him.

"Come on, come on!" Lucy shouted. She nervously paced around the kitchen. "You should have landed by now," she said anxiously.

Mark remained still as possible, as he listened to every sound she made. He visualized her every move. He was also anxiously awaiting Leo's arrival. He didn't know how he would react, but he would remain as still as possible until the perfect time.

The shrill sound of Lucy's cell phone ringing filled the

restaurant and echoed throughout the empty kitchen.

"Hello, brother?" Lucy's tone was overly excited.

"Oh, thank God! …. You have the address with you or do you need it? Your almost here then! ….. I can't wait to see you, too! Okay, have the cab driver bring you around back. My driver will pay him and he'll escort you in …. Great! Bye, bye!" Lucy squealed.

Lucy began skipping around like a school girl. She hummed to herself and sang something cheerful. Mark heard a refrigerator door open and the clinking of glasses.

"Was she celebrating?" The thought made him cringe. Mark was shaking with anger.

This was going to be harder than he thought. It was going to take a lot of patience to sit still and keep quiet. He knew he needed to keep his cool, now more than ever, and remain composed so he didn't blow this opportunity. Mark took slow, deep breaths, to calm down. After all, Leo wasn't even there yet. This was only the beginning.

The sound of Lucy's high heels, clicked throughout the dining hall. Mark thought she was probably looking out the windows. With a huff of excitement, she abruptly clomped back into the kitchen. The moment Mark heard the back door open; he felt the hair on the back of his neck stand up. He slowly rotated his shoulders one at a time and rolled his head from side to side to ease the rising of uncomfortable tension. It was an unmistakable warning. Leo was here.

"Tina, baby! My Lord, you look stunning!" Leo said. His voice didn't sound at all familiar to Mark. That was odd. Mark was almost disappointed that he didn't recognize it.

There was a long silence, and he heard Lucy begin to weep.

"I'm so glad you made it, Leo! I've waited for so long, for this very moment... where I could hold my baby brother in my arms again," Lucy cried.

Mark fumed with rage. He was unsure of how much of this he could take. Mark would NEVER be able to see his sister or his daughter alive again, let alone hug them! Heat rose up in him... burning his ears and flushing his cheeks. His resentment towards them alone, boiled the blood that his darkened heart now sent coursing through his veins.

He fantasized about putting his hands around their necks and squeezing the miserable life out of each of them.

Clenching his fists, he forced himself to remain still and silent. He remembered his training from the Gulf War. "Shut off all emotion, and keep your mind on the physical task at hand, then do it. Get it done." He silently chanted this in his mind, over and over, like a mantra.

He closed his eyes in the dark and refocused his mind. The time was coming.... It just wasn't right now. He would wait for his intuition to prep him for the right moment, the infamous click.

"It's so good to see you too, sissy, outside the prison even! I'm not sure what to call you. Do I call you Lucy or can I call you

Tina?" Leo asked lightheartedly.

"I love it when you call me, sissy! You can call me Tina, you can call me whatever you'd like," she laughed.

"I know it seems a bit silly to have changed my name, but it was all necessary, and I would do it again if I had to," she said proudly.

"You will be so proud of me, Leo, once you hear of all I've done for you. I have dedicated the last ten years of my life to bringing our family closer to justice for what that little imbecile did to you, TO US!" Lucy quickly turned nasty.

"I AM proud of you Sissy. I am so lucky to have a sister like you to love me and care so much about the family," Leo sounded emotional.

"The hardest part, I thought… has turned out to be the easiest," Lucy continued bragging about her accomplishments.

"Controlling Nick, was much simpler than I had originally thought," she said.

It sounded, to Mark, like they were moving the metal folding chairs over to the steel prepping table in the middle of the kitchen.

"This Nick character… how is that situation playing out?" Leo inquired.

"Like a dream," Lucy said confidently.

"He's so screwed up on drugs; he tried to blow his brains out last night. Can you believe it?" Lucy asked coolly.

"His dim-wit of a wife supposedly "caught" us yesterday and left him. I decided it was time to let him go anyway. It worked out best for us. I don't need to be involved in there drama. I figured I'd let him hang himself... I just didn't think he would literally try it," she laughed wickedly.

"You've got to tell me, sissy. I'm dying to know. How on earth did you manage to get him to kill Allie?" Leo asked, sounding amused.

"How do you think? Look at me, it was a piece of cake! I could get him to do anything I wanted," Lucy laughed, cynically.

"I gave him what all immature little boys want," Lucy grinned devilishly, "a little attention and some CANDY on the side. The man is a crack head. I got him hooked up with my housekeeper and her contacts. I paid for it, and bribed him with it. It worked to my advantage that he already hated Mark with a passion... and was always SO jealous of him, that it wasn't hard to turn him against the girl too. He was even jealous of the brat for spending time with Julie," Lucy continued to explain.

"I black mailed him with the drugs and our affair, if he started to talk crazy, like, he didn't want to do it, or he wasn't sure anymore.... I might have threatened him with our family reputation, once or twice," Lucy smiled slyly.

"I convinced him that it was Mark, who would be poisoned that night. He wouldn't have had anything to do with the girl's death. I said I would handle it, and I did. So, with that "crystal violet" compound I had told you about, I had it mixed into the frosting that was put on the girl's cake, like I told you. But he had no clue, that what he was really doing was poisoning Allie instead of Mark. He couldn't wait to give Mark his just desserts! He was a nervous wreck that night. He couldn't handle the pressure or the excitement," she light heartedly continued.

"The motive won't be hard for the pigs to prove. Plus, he's already confessed to poisoning the girl. Anything else he says, I'll deny and call him a lunatic. What difference does it make who I sleep with anyway, that doesn't make me a murderer," Lucy grabbed the wine bottle and poured them a glass.

"Nick's reputation is already tarnished and he'll be labeled as nothing but a low life, druggy, murderer. You know how they get treated in the system," Lucy paused. She glanced up at Leo to gauge his response. She feared she may have overstepped. "I'm sorry, I didn't mean that you-"

"I understand. I know all too well, actually," Leo said solemnly.

Lucy continued.

"That night, I covered my tracks well. I deliberately hired triple the normal amount of people to help out with the silly, over the top, birthday party. I thought it would confuse the cops when they started to investigate. Maybe send them off with a few false leads."

She mocked the scenario in a baby voice.

"But when "Princess Allie" fell... after eating the poisoned apple... the commotion from the guests was like nothing I could have ever expected," Lucy said. "Nick apologized profusely for his mistake. I told him that it would work out better for us this way."

She put her hand to her heart and smiled sweetly at Leo, "I promised him that he would have money to support us and we could run away together, as soon as he got rid of Julie and that I wanted you to have Mark all to yourself, anyway." She mocked. "I can't wait to hear what you have planned for him, by the way" she squealed.

Mark was clenching his jaw so tight... he tasted blood. He channeled his anger into his hands, as they remained bawled into fists. "SOON," he thought.

He continued to listen, until the perfect moment would come when he would walk into that kitchen....

"Oh, you'll see," Leo said cheerfully.

"If only you could have been here that night! This place was a zoo. I thought it was never going to end!" Lucy boasted. "There were people crying and running around frantically," she said animatedly.

"What did you end up doing that night? Surely you didn't go to the hospital with them, did you?" Leo asked, interested.

"I went with Dom and stood by his side, of course. I put on a sad, yet supportive face and got out of there as soon as I could," She said.

"He played his part exceptionally well. Just like I knew he would. Dom was absolutely mortified and was SOOO concerned for Mark!" Lucy laughed again. "Thank God he was there to handle everything and control the situation. That's true to Dom's fashion," Lucy said dramatically.

Mark was absolutely certain that Dom was a part of this conspiracy now. He obviously knew it was a possibility, but never fully accepted it. It hurt a little more to hear it than he anticipated.

"How did you ever find Vinny, in the first place? Or, excuse me... Mark Anderson," Leo smiled.

"I already told you all that, don't you remember?" Lucy was confused. Maybe she hadn't, she thought.

"Yeah, you mentioned it, but I don't think I understood it right. Did you say you married a cop in the Witness Protection Agency?" Leo asked.

"I sure did, brother. That kind of information is hard to get when you have no money... I just had to get creative with the right person. I rode that out a little bit, and once I got what I wanted, I said, 'Honey... I'm going for a walk, don't wait up,'" Lucy laughed.

"Mazzo was his name. He was a dirty cop and a shitty husband. It was easy to move on to Dom, with his successful restaurant and everything. It was much more exciting. It's been a wonderful working environment ever since," she joked. "It kind of reminded me of the good ole days with Pop in the family restaurant... you know, before Joey was killed," she said sadly.

"I think about those days too," Leo said sadly. "So what's next, Sissy? What's left in your bag of tricks?" he mused.

Lucy delighted in the fact that her brother was teasing her the way he used to when they were younger, when things were simpler.

"Well, Dom is gone. He left right after speaking to the lawyer this morning. He's been taking care of his sister, Anita. So there's really no need to bother him with anything right now," Lucy said as she stood from the table.

"After you kill Mark, I think it's time we take a trip to the bank and retrieve the contents of my safe deposit box," Lucy chimed. "And then it's first class baby, wherever we want to go!" Lucy smiled in a childlike manner and stretched her arms out like an airplane.

"So, what about Mark, how are you going to do it?" Lucy inquired.

Leo paused. He didn't quite know what to say.

Lucy's arms plopped back to her sides. She tilted her head and looked down at her brother, decisively.

"I think Mark needs to continue living his life... knowing that he has lost everything, just as we have," Leo said, sounding unsure.

"What? That's your plan?" Lucy sounded let down. "I'll kill him if you want me to do it."

Leo quickly stood up and embraced his sister, lingering for a moment.

"You know I love you, right?" Leo said sincerely.

Their embrace was quickly broken off, as Lucy heard the swish of the double doors and the sound of someone entering the kitchen behind her.

CHAPTER 17

SNAKE EYES

"Dom," Lucy looked terrified. "What are you doing here?" she asked.

Leo cautiously stepped away from Lucy and took a few steps back towards the end of the metal table.

Mark listened intently. Waiting for the right moment to come out of hiding, he noiselessly removed the tile and set it off to the side, remaining silent.

Dom slowly walked into the kitchen. He kept his eyes on Lucy as he grabbed a nearby stool and propped the door open with it.

"Well, hello! I was looking for you, my dear," Dom said, in a matter-of-fact way.

"You weren't home, so I drove by the restaurant to see if you had come to work, perhaps. And... here you are," he smiled and bowed his head.

"You seem surprised to see me, in my own restaurant nonetheless," Dom chuckled.

Leo calmly stood and stared at Dom with reverence in his eyes.

"I thought you were with Anita. I wasn't expecting you to be HERE all of the sudden, that's all!" Lucy said disgruntled.

With a much softer tone, Lucy regained her composure.

"Well, it's about time that you two meet, face to face. Dom, this is my older brother, Leo. Leo, this is my husband, Dom Angelo," Lucy said respectfully.

Leo nodded his head courteously toward Dom.

Mark inaudibly descended from the ceiling in the storage room, quietly landing with a soft thud as his rubber soled boots hit the ground. No one heard a thing, as they were deep in they own discussion, completely unaware of his presence. He gently unsnapped his holster buttons, and withdrew his two guns. He was ready. He hadn't felt the instinctual sign, but his heart had told him that the time had come.

Dom knowingly looked at Lucy, and said, "Yes, darling. I know who he is. We have come to know each other, very well, these last few months."

Lucy looked suddenly perplexed. She was confused.

"I should have known," Mark said loudly as he slowly walked out of the dark storage room with both guns drawn. The gun on the left was aimed at Dom's head, with the gun on the right, pointed at Leo's. Everyone was extremely surprised to see Mark suddenly standing there. Lucy backed up and reached out for her brother, who instinctively put his arm around her. They held each other with fear in their eyes.

"Marko, put the guns down," Dom ordered adamantly. "Please."

Mark glared at Dom with such hatred in his eyes. "You are in NO position to tell me, what I should or shouldn't do," Mark spoke slowly and clearly. Dom took a step back, astonished.

"We need to have a discussion, you and I. It's very important that you trust me right now," Dom responded.

"The only person in this room, that I trust right now, is me," Mark spoke through clenched teeth. "And even I don't fully know what I'm capable of doing right now."

Mark shifted his glare to Leo, who stood motionless with a frightened Lucy. He looked at Mark, like he had just seen a ghost.

Leo gives Dom, a confused look and tightens his grip on Lucy, holding her now, to the side of him in a protective stance.

"Now you know how it feels, Leo… to shield your sister, from a lunatic with a gun," Mark said with a sinister grin.

"Please, Marko, I beg of you to put the gun away. You need to listen to what I have to say," Dom said firmly.

"No, YOU need to listen to what I have to say! Why don't YOU give me the answers I want to hear, Dom, since your so fucking chatty! We all know you had a hand, in all of this!" Marks rage was unyielding. All he wanted was for Dom to say ONE incriminating thing on that tape, so he could put a bullet in his head.

Dom shook his head in disagreement. "No, Marko. You don't understand, you're wrong about me," Dom's eyes pleaded with him.

"Listen to him, Mark," said a familiar voice, just outside the door.

Williams was suddenly visible, just inside the door. He stepped in slowly around the stool that Dom had propped the door open with. Williams had his gun drawn also… and had it pointed in Lucy and Leo's direction.

"Williams? What in the HELL are you doing here?" Mark asked abruptly. Mark became increasingly alarmed.

"Forgive me, my friend, I couldn't let you do this alone. Mark, don't do anything you might regret. You need to seriously keep your wits about you… because shit's about to get crazy," Williams' gaze shifted from Mark to Leo.

"Someone needs to start talking and tell me what the fuck is going on," Mark yelled, "NOW!"

"Wait, you know what? I want to hear you say it, Dom. Tell me how you helped kill your god-daughter! I want to know every detail of your devious plan," Mark demanded.

Mark had no more self-control left. The tension in that room, was only adding fuel to his fire. He didn't want Williams to ever be a part of this, or to see him this way. Mark had come too far... so he wasn't going to stop now.

"I wouldn't do such a thing. I love Allie," Dom said diligently.

Lucy scoffed loudly. "Oh, my God! He doesn't know a thing you stupid imbecile!" she spat. "It was all me!" she yelled proudly. "You think only HE is capable of such orchestration?" Lucy seemed offended.

Mark quickly glanced at Dom, who watched Lucy with disgust.

Lucy tried to step towards Mark, but Leo had a good hold of her. Williams flinched.

Mark focused on her again.

"You would FIRST, have to understand what you have done to me and my family to truly appreciate all the time and effort I have spent, waiting, and planning... to see you just like this!" She pointed at Mark. "So lost, scared, and broken..."

Lucy smiled maniacally, as she reveled in her self-justifiable madness.

"After Leo was sentenced and sent away to prison for the murders he didn't commit, my father had a massive heart attack and died! I watched my mother struggle. She had to sell the restaurant to pay the mountain of debt that she accumulated!" Lucy screeched.

Leo's face contorted. He closed his eyes and held on to his trembling sister.

"Staying home and caring for her wasn't enough. There was nothing I could do to help her. She told me she lost both her sons that night," Lucy turned and looked at Leo, speaking directly to him now. "She slowly sank into depression… and ate a bottle of pills for dinner one night, and never woke up," Lucy admitted.

Leo was stunned. He had never known that this was how his mother had truly passed.

Everyone remained silent listening to her ranting.

Marks grip became tighter on the gun he aimed at Lucy. "Say the wrong thing and you're dead, bitch," he thought to himself.

Lucy turned back around and faced Mark once again. "I alone had to avenge my families dishonor. I knew then, that I needed to exact revenge on you for taking all our hopes and dreams, and throwing it away, like garbage. It was because of YOU, that Alice and Joey died… It was because of YOU, that Leo had to pull a gun to protect him against you that night. YOU who set him up with your dirty cop friends that protected you in court! YOU, who put him away with your lie's!" She was shaking uncontrollably, her eyes wild with fury. "The judge sentenced us all that day… to a life of hell… and some of us… to uncertain death!"

Lucy was choking on her words now, crying uncontrollably. "I wanted to show my brother, that we can have our honor back and start over! All I wanted was to make him proud of me!" Lucy turned quickly into Leo and sobbed into his shoulder.

Mark saw how fragile Lucy's mental state really was. She was a psychopath at best... but he had no idea how delusional she was. She was pointing the finger at the wrong person. It was Leo who needed to come clean to his dear sister, who spent a large chunk of her life, fighting for his lost integrity. All of her devious efforts were because of his lies.

Mark glanced at Dom who now stared at Lucy with sympathy in his eyes.

Tears fell from Leo's eyes as he whispered into Lucy's ear. No one could hear what he said over her crying and carrying on.

"I'm so sorry... it's the truth. Look at me Tina!" Leo said loudly. He continued to hold on to her as she struggled to get free.

"No! It can't be... you wouldn't have done that!" Lucy exclaimed.

"It was Mark, not you that killed them!" Lucy's reality was beginning to spiral out of control.

"It's true." Leo looked at Mark with sincerity. "I killed Joey and Alice.... and their unborn baby, that night."

Mark didn't want to hear this. Whatever Leo was trying to accomplish by telling him the truth... it wasn't going to work.

Nothing was going to soften his anger. It was too late for retribution.

"I could care less about your stupid ideas, or sympathy's…. I know for a fact that my daughter is DEAD because of all of you! Only Lucy has the gall to fess up to it! My innocent baby, that did nothing wrong to deserve any of this, is gone!" Mark squeezed both of his guns. He wasn't wasting any more time. There had been enough talking.

Williams' gun arm was shaking now… but his gun remained pointed at Lucy and Leo.

"Mark, don't do it! PLEASE, let Dom explain," Williams could feel the situation crumbling fast.

"Why don't you just let me do, what I have to… remember that part of our agreement? This is that time when you were supposed to walk away, and you didn't, so shut the fuck up and man up!" Mark grumbled under his breathe.

"To hell with our agreement, I'm here to keep you from making a terrible mistake. You're not a cold blooded killer, Mark. Not like them. Are you capable? Yes. Is it necessary? NO," Williams' arm shook as he kept aim on Lucy, who now stared blankly at Mark.

Mark remembered what Julie had said earlier, "Someone could get hurt, or worse, killed. Enough innocent people have died already."

Dom spoke just then and broke Marks concentration.

"I had nothing to do with her horrible game. I did not kill Allie, nor did I have anyone do it for me," Dom said truthfully.

"Leo, put the cuffs on her now, please," Dom ordered. Lucy turned and looked at Leo with unbelieving fear in her eyes. He took out a pair of handcuffs, and clapped it across her left wrist. He twisted her hands quickly behind her back, and fastened the other to join her other wrist.

"What are you doing, brother?" Lucy was awestruck. "Leo, answer me! I demand an explanation!" she cried.

Dom spoke loudly over Lucy's pleas.

"Three months ago, I was contacted by Leo Vanzetti. I went to see him, and that is when he told me that his sister, Tina, was my Lucy, and she had a deadly plan in effect. He couldn't let it happen. He wanted her to be put into a place, where she could be taken care of properly for her severe mental issues. I believed this man to be telling the truth," Dom quickly, yet precisely explained.

"I immediately started investigating the accusation, and discovered her affair with Nick. The rest of the design unraveled quickly. I had to act fast, and discreetly. I couldn't tell you a thing, Marko. Lucy's plan had to be thwarted, but she couldn't think it was in any danger. She had to believe that it all went off without a hitch," Dom spoke directly to Mark. "Leo has cooperated fully and willingly."

Lucy screamed.

"LIE'S! Leo you wouldn't do this to me, tell me he's lying!"

Lucy shrieked at him.

"He's telling the truth," Leo said, with watery eyes. He looked at Mark when he spoke.

"You think I'm going to fall for this sob story? You don't think I know what's going on here? You're all turning against her; you're flipping on her, because she's the stupid broad that admitted to everything already! REAL classy guys, throw the crazy lady under the bus!" Mark laughed. "Do you believe this crock, Williams?" Mark asked sarcastically.

Williams nodded his head.

"It's the absolute truth. It's all part of another F.B.I investigation. It stems all the way back… starting with the Agent who gave away your personal information and many others who are in the Witness Protection Program," he stated.

Williams lowered his gun, relieving his aching arms, and proving that the threat was gone.

"This stand-off needs to end, Mark. No one is in any danger here. The only threat is you, just put the guns down," Williams said sincerely.

"I'm an F.B.I informant," Dom admitted. "Once I began investigating Lucy, we discovered her connection to the pre-existing case, regarding the witness protection breach. We, the F.B.I and Leo here, decided to work together… and quickly. There was no time for finesse. We couldn't jeopardize the Federal case," Dom looked over at a stunned Lucy.

"Williams just found out about an hour ago. I couldn't tell you, Marko. They wouldn't let me. It damn near killed me not to. Believe me when I say… that it's the hardest thing I've ever had to do in my LIFE!" Dom pleaded.

Marks arms swayed and shook with fatigue, but he wouldn't put the guns down. "You couldn't try to save her though? You just led my innocent daughter, out to slaughter…. just so you didn't have to COMPROMISE your investigation!" Mark felt sick to his stomach. "You're sadistic, all of you," Marks head swooned. He was struggling to rationalize.

"No wonder you were so eager to help with everything… her burial, the autopsy, everything! You felt guilty… you were trying to ease your guilty conscience about what you had done! Did it work? Did it make you feel better when you paid her funeral bills?" Mark felt his adrenaline return. He then put both guns on Dom.

Williams quickly drew on Mark.

"Mark, please… there's so much more that needs explaining. Come on buddy, I know your paranoid as heck right now, and you have every right to be! But I need you to realize that what we're saying sounds crazy… but is 100% true," Williams begged.

"I don't care. I don't care about any of this anymore," Mark mumbled.

"You're right!" Dom yelled and got his attention. "Marko, your right, It wasn't easy to go through, but it was necessary. I will explain more to you soon, but the next words I speak to you are very important. You must trust that I'm telling you the truth. I don't deserve it…. I know. But I need you to believe in me," Dom insisted.

Mark went wild. His eyes were darker than death itself.

"YOUR truth and MY truth are different, aren't they? SWEAR! SWEAR on my dead daughter's body, that you're telling me the truth!" Mark yelled ferociously. "SAY IT!"

"I can't swear to that Marko… I can't! She is not dead, she is ALIVE!" Dom finally exclaimed.

Mark and Lucy stared at Dom in disbelief for what seemed like minutes, but were only seconds.

"What?" Mark looked at Williams who had once again, lowered his gun. Williams had a look of pure relief on his face.

"You're LYING!" Mark shouted. The room began to spin; he was dizzy and going into shock.

"She's alive and well! I promise you," Dom reassured him.

"That can't be… I saw her laid out in the… the hospital," Mark felt his sanity slipping away. He didn't know what was real anymore. This revelation shocked him to his core.

"I know this a lot to take in, just try to stay calm. You'll get all of your answers soon enough. Just put the guns down," Williams added.

Mark felt his arms go numb. Maybe they fell on their own

out of pure exhaustion, or maybe he just gave up and dropped them.

Williams caught hold of Mark's arm, as his body slumped to the floor. Williams sat beside him on the ground, amidst a whirl wind of police activity. He safely secured his weapons and put the safety's back on, putting them in Marks holsters. They watched in silence as agents poured in, taking away a screaming, hysterical Lucy. Leo walked out, with his head hung low, not looking up at anyone.

"Everything's alright now, you'll see," Williams assured Mark. A feeling of relief washed over his body, triggering an instinct. This familiar feeling made him think that this could be real.

"Where is she?" Mark looked bewildered at Williams.

"She's been at Anita's, all weekend long," Williams assured him.

Dom, who had been dealing with Fed's and Police outside in the hallway, now came in and knelt beside Mark on the floor in the kitchen. Williams got up to give them privacy.

"He's not talking much. I think he's in shock," Williams mentioned. "I'm going out to the dining area.

Mark asked Dom. "How could you of done this?"

"We drugged her wine. There was never any poison in the icing... we got to that in time," Dom looked at Marks blank expression as he began to stare at the floor, and continued.

"Allie responded differently to it than we thought… I didn't expect her to stay out as long as she had.   She didn't suffer a second though… she doesn't remember a thing either. Her breathing was so shallow, that it appeared she wasn't breathing when you saw her at the hospital. The doctors and the nurses… they were all F.B.I… stop me when you want, it's just all pouring out of me now, Marko…. Will you ever forgive me?" Dom asked sincerely. "This is the worst thing I have ever done to anyone. I'm so sorry for causing you this pain and heartache, it's the ultimate kind of betrayal," he acknowledged sullenly.

Mark didn't answer him. He just leaned his back up against the wall, and put his head between his knees.

Dom realized that Mark wasn't going to respond to him just yet… but there would hopefully be plenty of time for explanations later.

Williams poked his head into the kitchen entry way.

"Someone couldn't wait any longer to see you, and I think we can all agree, that it's been long enough," Williams said. He held open the double doors.

Mark couldn't believe his eyes… his mouth fell open. He felt as though he were frozen to the floor, unable to budge.

"Dad?" Allie came in searching for him. Spotting him quickly, she ran to where Mark was and skidded to the floor onto her knees, wrapping her arms around him immediately. "Dad, are you okay?" she cried.

Marks eyes welled up with tears that flowed freely down his face. His eyes were fixed open. He put his arms around her, still unbelieving that this was actually happening. He had to be dreaming, he thought.

"Allie, baby girl," Mark closed his eyes and held her to him tightly. She wasn't a dream, she was very real.

"Let me look at you," he could barely manage to speak. He wanted to see that she was whole.

Mark held her tear streaked face in his hands and brushed her hair back. He never thought that in a million years he would be able to look in her eyes again. She smiled at him with the same crooked grin she always has.

"Oh, dear GOD, thank you! You're alive," he wept. "Thank you Jesus…. I don't deserve this. Thank you, Jesus!" Mark prayed over his daughter.

"I'm okay, dad. Really I am," She assured him. "Are you alright? I know you were TOTALLY about to blast some people away a few minutes ago," she laughed through her tears.

"I'm so sorry, dad! I wanted to tell you sooner," she hugged him tighter.

He got up onto his knees and grabbed her again, kissing the top of her head. "I'll be alright, honey. I'm just not EVER letting you out of my sight, again!"

Mark continued to pray over his daughter, and praise Jesus for his miracles. Allie had never heard her father pray before, but she liked it. Finally, she felt safe and totally secure in his arms, thankful that this ordeal was finally over.

"Thank you, Jesus," she whispered, smiling.

Allie may have missed him all weekend, but Mark had missed her for a life time.

CHAPTER 18

BIGGER FISH

Allie and Mark slowly emerged from the kitchen.

They had been talking; going back and forth on whether Allie could make a phone call without the Fed's approval. She knew that many people would want to know just what the heck had happened for her to rise from the grave. So they discussed the most appropriate thing she could say.

"I know exactly what to say, but due to an ongoing Federal investigation, I'm not allowed to go into details," Allie confirmed with a know-it-all smile.

Mark reluctantly agreed to let Allie call Jen. Allie sat down at the nearest table, eager to use Marks cell phone. She couldn't wait any longer to tell Jen she was alive and well. Mark listened nearby, and walked over to Williams, who was leaning against the wall.

"The media is going to have a field day with this. The Fed's are going to have to give them something to go on," Williams rubbed his forehead, massaging his headache.

"What all does she know?" Mark asked, nodding towards Allie.

"She knows that Lucy and Nick turned out to be bad people,

and they tried to hurt you both. She knows that her and Dom kept secrets from you, and everyone else. They were trying to do the right thing by the Fed's," Williams paused.

"She's very bright, Mark. She has handled all of this surprisingly well. I think the hardest part for her, was letting people think that she was… well, dead," he said poignantly.

"What do you mean by all that? Are you trying to tell me that she knew about this charade, and that she's a part of it?" Mark was getting angry again.

"Yes, apparently so; she has signed all the paperwork and cooperated fully, just as she agreed to," Williams carefully explained. "She was working with the F.B.I, Dad."

"That's ridiculous, she may be eighteen, but she's still just a little girl. How could they take advantage of her like that?" Mark was beyond pissed. "I get that there was never any poison, and she had a sleeping pill, but what if something went wrong with the pill? Didn't Dom say she reacted differently to that?" Mark looked sternly at Williams. "Why wasn't I brought in on this, before my daughter? Was she recruited?"

"I don't have the answers to that, my friend. I wish I did," Williams said truthfully.

"Basically, the F.B.I. used my family as bait, to catch a bigger fish, didn't they?" Mark said frankly.

"Basically, yeah," Williams agreed.

"I don't understand why Allie would go along with any of this. It doesn't make any sense," Mark was puzzled.

Mark was very tired and his voice was weak.

"I don't know either, Mark. It's all crazy to me. I've never seen an investigation conducted like this. I would be less than understanding as well," Williams agreed.

"Something like this, I wouldn't be surprised if the C.I.A was backing it... just to get the so-called, bigger fish," Williams speculated.

"The nerve of the F.B.I. is absolutely incredible. I still can't fully wrap my head around all that has happened. It's going to take some time to rethink all of the events, and try to see something I didn't see before...-" Mark's mind was reeling from the days confusing events.

"The investigation is over, Mark. What the heck am I even talking about? There never was an investigation for us to solve. All though we damn near had this figured out in two days, didn't we?" Williams and Mark both laughed and smiled at the notion.

"Maybe, you should just take your daughter, and go home. Give it a few days, and we'll definitely call you and keep you updated on everything. Okay? For real this time! Just be the "grateful, doting father", and nothing more. Get some sleep for goodness sake, you look like crap!" Williams patted his friend on the shoulder.

"Yeah, I suppose." Mark grinned.   "I don't think I want to get involved in it anyway. All these years I've tried to shield Allie, to protect her from knowing the awful truth and here it all is, laid out for her to see. I never wanted for her to get involved in anything like this. I'm so thankful to God that I've got everything that's important to me now. That's all that matters," he watched as Allie put the cell phone down.

Allie stood up and walked over to her father and Detective Williams, and hugged her father's arm, grabbing a hold of it tightly.

"Allie, I'm not sure if you've formerly met him or not, but this is Detective Williams," Mark said. "He was your personal homicide detective," Mark grinned.

"Hi, there, I know that you've helped my dad quite a bit over the last couple of days. Thank you so much… for everything. It's so nice to meet you!" Allie smiled warmly.

"It's very nice to meet you too, Miss Allie. The pleasure was all mine," Williams looked into the eyes of the young girl he fought so hard to defend. "It's not every day that a Homicide Detective… gets to meet his victim," he said, deeply touched.

Allie grabbed his hand with both of hers and held it for a moment, shaking it, respectively.

"You're a very strong willed young woman, to have gone through this ordeal as well as you have," Williams applauded her. "I think I might know who you get it from."

"Thank you Detective Williams," Allie said sincerely.

Mark's eyes squinted, as he thought of what she might have gone through.

"You know why I did it, don't you Dad? Do you have any idea at all?" Allie turned towards Mark, looking at him seriously.

"I don't actually. I have many questions Allie, but I would love to hear whatever you have to say," Mark answered as he reached out to smooth her hair around her face.

"I did this to end it, once and for all. To me, this meant… no more hiding for either of us. I felt that it was an opportunity to expose the secrets that we have hidden for so long. It's all over now and there's no more wondering "What if," Allie looked at her father very earnestly.

Mark now saw his little girl, as the strong, beautiful woman that she had become. He watched her face, and listened to how passionately she talked about what she was able to accomplish. How deeply proud and confident she was.

"I believe Dom got involved when he discovered that another agent had talked to me already. He tried to talk me out of it, but it was no use. I told him to work with me or against me. What he didn't expect, was my own, personal vendetta, to have all of these questions answered that I have had on my mind… and in my dreams, for as long as I can remember," Allie painfully disclosed.

"I wanted to know all of it, and I wanted to stop it from happening again."

Mark suddenly understood her reasoning. He continued to listen carefully, not saying a word, and letting her say her peace.

"I knew it would hurt you, momentarily... but I didn't think it would have lasted for two whole days. Something went wrong, and we couldn't find you. I also knew there was a risk to drinking the wine with the sleeping agent. But it was my idea, and my decision to make. Please don't hate Dom for it," Allie pleaded.

"Allie, I know that your eighteen now, and that you're more than capable of making your own decisions... but there is more than a miscommunication between Dom and I. Don't you worry about that that. I'll deal with that on my own time," Mark stated.

Williams stood by silently listening.

"But, what did you mean by something went wrong? You tried to contact me sooner?" Mark inquired.

"Yes! We couldn't find you after you left Julie's last night. You didn't go where you were guys were supposed to or something. Not that I'm complaining, too much," Allie smirked.

"Then this morning after Captain Haddock was "finally" briefed by the Fed's... you disappeared again! Only Dom guessed where you might be... and then he called Detective Williams," Allie gestured at Williams.

Marks mind was too frazzled to think all of this through. He HAD hid Julie so no one could find her... and he was with her last night.

Williams intervened.

"This brings ME to ask a question of my own... Where on earth is Julie? We found her car at the hotel she was SUPPOSED to be at... but she's not there," Williams looked exasperated.

Mark laughed, and said, "I guess it's safe to bring her out of hiding now, isn't it? How about you give us a ride to pick up her car, and then I'll show you?" Mark asked.

"What are we waiting for?" Williams responded.

Mark quickly reached out and grabbed William's arm, surprising him.

"Thank you for fighting for me. It couldn't have been easy. I appreciate what you've done for me and my family. Thank you, brother, it won't be forgotten," Mark said sincerely.

Williams pulled him in for a quick shoulder hug, and smacked him firmly on the back.

"Anytime, brother, let's go get Julie and get you guys home. You deserve it," Williams declared.

"You're on to something," Mark agreed, smiling.

"You got the phone?" Mark asked Allie.

"Yeah, it's right here," she said, as they walked out of the restaurant.

"Why don't you call Julie and tell her to pack up her things.

Let her know we'll be at the hotel in ten minutes," Mark said as they walked across the parking lot.

"No, way I'm not calling her! It would freak her out big time. It would almost be better to just show her in person, so she doesn't think it's a cruel joke or something. It took me like five whole minutes just to convince Jen it wasn't a prank call," Allie said seriously.

"This whole thing has been a bit of a cruel joke," Mark thought.

"Alright, I understand. Let's go get her and take her home," Mark decided.

"Home, like to OUR home?" Allie asked excited.

"Yeah, maybe, what do you think about that?" Mark stopped and anxiously looked at his daughter.

"It's about time!" Allie winked and smiled.

CHAPTER 19

HUMBLE PIE

Julie turned off the television and tossed the remote onto the hotel bed. She sat down in the chair by the window and curled her legs up to her chest, wrapping her arms around her knees. Perhaps she would watch the cars in the parking lot again and people watch some more. This hiding business was boring as hell.

Any other time in her life, she would have loved a whole day of doing nothing, but all she thought about was Mark and Allie. Julie couldn't imagine ever recovering from the loss of such a sweet soul like Allies. She thought about Allie a lot that day. Julie remembered this one particular time, back when she had finally received her Masters from college. Allie had this "great idea" to surprise her and they all went to Skate World. Mark was so wobbly on his skates. Allie danced circles around him, holding on to his hands.

Julie couldn't remember having laughed so hard before that. Nick had thought the whole thing was childish and faked a headache, so he could leave early. Remembering Nick made her stomach turn. This was still one of Julie's favorite memories though. It always made her smile and filled her heart with complete joy. Instead of smiling now, Julie's mouth tightened up into a frown. Tears filled up her eyes and now leaked out the corners, trickling down her face. She knew that without Allie and Mark, she would never feel that joy again.

Julie now wondered if she would ever see Mark again. She was very worried about him. So many things went through her mind. Sometimes, she would get so worked up about it, she would think about taking off and going to look for him. She even kept her bag packed and ready to go just in case. But she knew that leaving wouldn't be a good idea. Mark didn't want her to find him. Whatever his plan was, it didn't seem like it would end well for anybody. All she could do now was hope and pray for some divine miracle.

So, instead, Julie sat in her chair and gazed out the window, watching the cars pull in and out from the main street. "Nice blinker buddy," she commented.

"Yep, the person behind you is psychic; they knew exactly what you were going do," Julie criticized out loud.

"And to think that all this time, we've had it all wrong…" she thought. "Dogs hate stupid drivers and can't communicate their disdain, so they chase and bark at them instead. Hmm," she said sarcastically.

Julie spotted a familiar looking black, S.U.V. pulling into the parking lot. Then she saw that her car was following right behind it.

"No way, it's Mark and Detective Williams!" Julie exclaimed. She jumped up and ran to her stuff on the bed. Shoving her sneakers quickly on to her feet, she went back to the window, looking down and around. She couldn't see where they had gone.

"I thought for sure that was Detective Williams and Mark coming to get me," She thought. Julie wasn't exactly looking forward to going back to her house, but this did mean that she could start to move on with her life.

She was anxious to find out what had gone on. Most of all, she was grateful that Mark was okay and about to walk through that door. One last glance in the bathroom and she was reassured that she had everything ready to go. Maybe one more check under the bed. You never know.

"What's taking so long? They must be checking out or something," she thought. She stood in the center of the room, near the foot of the bed and excitedly awaited her company. There was a rapid little knock at the door.

Julie pushed the thick metal lever down and pulled the door open.

A look of disbelief and shock swept over her smiling face, as she realized who was staring back at her. Mark stepped in and quickly grabbed Julie as she began to stumble backwards.

Julie shook her head as if to say, "No".

"Jules, it's ok. Yes, it's Allie…. She's alive and well," Mark sat her on the bed and held her, whispering in her ear.

"Everything's going to be alright."

"I told you this was a ridiculous idea!" Allie said, concerned for Julie. "What if she has heart failure or a seizure or something?"

Allie knelt down in front of Julie and touched her leg. "Hi, Julie, It's me. I have a lot of explaining to do, I know," Allie stated.

Williams came into the room, and shut the door behind him. He smiled at Julie, as she looked up at him blankly.

"I don't understand what's going on right now," Julie looked at Allie, but didn't know if it was really her that was looking back. Was this a figment of her imagination?

"You see her and hear her too, right?" Julie looked from Mark to Detective Williams.

Smiling, Williams nodded his head, reassuring her that it was indeed true.

Mark laughed, "Yes. We see her and hear her as well. Allie isn't dead Jule's. I know it's a shock, imagine my surprise! I thought I had lost my mind for good," Mark said truthfully.

Julie cautiously reached out and touched Allies hand. It was warm. Nothing like when she had seen her in the hospital. She suddenly wrapped her arms around Allies neck and shoulders, squeezing her.

"It's you!" Julie cried. "Oh my goodness, I can't believe

you're alive! You are, you're really here and you're really breathing," Julie was slowly convinced.

"Yeah, I am!" Allie laughed. "Now that you know that I'm not a member of the undead zombie world, I should explain, or try to at least," Allie said sounding muffled.

Julie continued to hold on to her tight, running her hand down the back of Allies head and feeling her hair. "Oh, you silly girl, you scared me senseless," Julie wept.

Allie tried to sit next to her on the bed, as she awkwardly knelt in front of Julie. Mark slid off the bed and helped Allie get seated, considering Julie wasn't letting go anytime soon.

"It's okay, Julie, I'll tell you everything that happened," Allie couldn't help but cry. She was so moved by the emotion that poured out of Julie. Julie loved her so much, that was very apparent. But what was more obvious, was how much pain she knew she had caused her... all of them, really. The gravity of her fake death had much more emphasis than she could have ever imagined. She knew that now. Julie had also grieved very hard, and hurt so deeply over losing her. Just like her Dad.

"I'm so sorry, Julie. I never meant to hurt anyone. You were supposed to have found out sooner ... not that that really matters now," replied Allie.

"What do you mean?" Julie sat back, letting go of Allie. Julie wiped her face on her sleeve. "I saw you Allie, you weren't breathing. I couldn't believe it, you looked like you were sleeping.... But-"

Allie nodded her head as Julie made the realization. "I was," Allie answered.

Mark got up and grabbed a tissue box from the night table and after handing one to Allie and Julie first, he placed it between them on the bed.

"Well, the cake poisoning never happened. It was staged to throw off Lucy and Nick. It was to make Lucy think she succeeded in killing me. Dom put a sleeping pill in the wine I drank. It kept me out for quite a while and kept my breathing really shallow. There were real doctors around me, monitoring me. I was safe the whole time," Allie explained.

"Dom, he was behind this, for sure?" Julie looked really confused now.

"Yeah, he's an F.B.I. Informant. He was the one working with Leo Vanzetti to bust Lucy," Allie said, knowingly.

"What?" Julie looked at Mark.

"Okay, let's let Williams explain all that. Alright honey?" Mark said patting Allie's shoulder.

"Oh, right," Allie nodded.

Julie looked at Williams and raised her eyebrows, waiting to be filled in.

Silent until now, Williams tried to explain the situation more clearly.

"Uh, well. That's about right, actually," he loudly cleared his throat.

"It basically stems back to an ongoing investigation by the F.B.I. It was about bringing down a group of police officers who profited off of selling contact information of protected witnesses, like Mark and Allie. They're just a couple of cops, out of at least a hundred nationwide.

Lucy, A.K.A. Christina L. Mazzo, was able to get the "new" names, addresses and phone numbers of Mark and Allie, from a cop she was married to at the time, who was only one of a handful of bad cops in his precinct. They would sell private, classified information to the highest bidder.

Once Lucy got what she wanted, she left him one day, out of the blue, completely disappearing. She moved here under an alias, and spent many years carrying out this revenge plot against Mark and used Dom to get into their lives. Nick was also a pawn, if you will. She made him think he was killing Mark, instead. As you know, the rest of their relationship besides there intimacy, involved drugs and murder for hire. But when Lucy told her brother, Leo, what she was planning on doing for him, he contacted Dom and told him everything. As it turns out, Leo's led a legitimately reformed life behind bars and recognized his sister's mental instability. She had hoped this insane murder plot would make him happy and proud of her in the least. Allie's death was supposed to be a gift of sorts to him," Williams stated.

"That's sick," Julie said, disgusted.

"Dom, we now know, is in fact, an F.B.I. informant. He then took this information from Leo, and went to his superiors and it was then that they connected the dots. Allie cooperated with the F.B.I and they decided to let Lucy think she had done all of this, so that when confronted by Leo and Dom, they could get a full confession about everything, but that's not exactly how it ended up going down," Williams sighed.

Julie was fuming mad. She sat listening to this explanation, and was still disgusted. She bent her legs and her knees began to bounce.

"So the Fed's and Dom, get to decide to drug a young girl and let her father think she's dead for two days?" Julie sat up straighter on the edge of the bed. "All of this, in the name of justice? Lucy's not the only one playing head games, huh?" Julie added.

Mark looked at Julie, somewhat surprised by her reaction, but totally agreeing with her thought process. "God love you, woman," Mark said as he kissed her head.

"It was my decision, Jules. It was my idea, actually," Allie explained.

Allie looked directly at her father now. "An F.B.I agent named Mr. Slatter confronted me a day after my actual eighteenth birthday, and he told me I needed to go in and talk to him. He asked me questions about Lucy and Nick and told me what Leo did to Aunt Alice and her boyfriend. I didn't have anything different to tell them, but I offered to help any way I could. He was unsure of the investigations approach at the time and said that the both of us would be contacted," Allie continued.

"A week before the party, Dom asked if I would stop by the restaurant on my way home from school. So Jen took me and waited outside. He told me to stay away from Nick and Lucy as much as possible. I played dumb and asked him why, but he wouldn't tell me."

Allie swallowed hard, trying to vanquish the lump that was forming in her throat. She hated keeping these secrets from her father. It was time to let it out.

Mark stood still listening carefully. Just hearing that Agent Slatter talked to her behind his back, upset him. He nodded at Allie to continue. He wanted to hear this.

"I told Dom to tell me the truth. I said I was eighteen and that he should treat me like an adult. He said "NO," that he didn't want me involved in any of this, but I kept insisting that if he knew something about MY life, that I was more entitled to know about it... much more than he was," Allie sounded very convincing.

"So, I told him that I knew about the guy that killed Aunt Alice and her boyfriend. That's why we moved, I already knew that, but then he told me that he didn't know about any of that. But he was lying, I knew he was. Dom said that he was trying to protect us and the least we knew, the better off we would be. I told him he wasn't fooling me and he better tell me what the connection is, because I knew there was one. He just said, "The F.B.I is investigating and they would take care of everything. They would talk to all of us soon," Allie took a deep breath.

"Dom said he shouldn't have said anything to me and that it was a big mistake and he had already told me too much. But, I got persuasive. I'm not proud of this, but I told him that if he didn't tell me everything, that I would blow their entire investigation wide open. So, I told him that he better tell me, or I was going to tell my father and anybody else that would listen, including Lucy, that there was an F.B.I investigation. That's when I told him that I already had talked to Agent Slatter," Allie grimaced as she remembered how persistent she had been with Dom.

"He was pretty shocked to hear of this. I could tell he was upset, but not at me. He was upset that I had been approached by someone in the bureau."

Looking at Marks face, full of chagrin, he didn't like it either.

"That's when Dom told me he was an F.B.I informant and he could help protect us. He didn't know they had contacted me, until I told him. He knew things about the investigation that Slatter didn't mention and he told me about them. Like Lucy being Leo Vanzetti's sister. Nick was going to poison Dad's piece of cake on the night of the party and Lucy had ordered him to do it. This was her way of getting back at you for testifying against Leo, whom she thought was totally innocent. She told her brother about her plan and he decided to report it, by calling Dom," Allie looked down at the ground.

She knew that this was hard for her dad to hear her side of

things. Well, it was hard on all of them for that matter. She just didn't want to disappoint her dad, but she knew she needed to be honest. He could handle it, if it was the truth. Allie hoped that he would understand why she did what she did next.

Julie put her arm around Allies shoulder to encourage her to keep going. She knew this wasn't easy for her to reiterate. She had been through a lot too.

Allie closed her eyes and remembered the conversation.

"I then asked him, 'If fewer people, the better, know about this, the better off the investigation will be, right?'"

Dom said, "Yes."

"So I had an idea. I told him to make her think she's done it. Let her go boast and brag about it to her brother when he gets out. Make him wear a wire. If he's really a changed man and wants to help by doing the right thing, then he'll get it all on tape. There's your confession. That would put her away for good and keep her from coming back again."

Allie's voice choked up. She took a moment and continued.

"Dom rejected the idea at first, but I told him I would go to Slatter if he didn't give it a shot. So, he thought about it. He called someone on the phone and spoke quietly. Whoever it was thought it was a brilliant plan. But the problem was that Dom didn't know how to stage something like that without everyone being involved."

"It would be too risky for the girl," Dom told the person on the phone.

"I realized it was Slatter on the line. Agent Slatter told Dom that only I needed to be in on it and the other agents of course… and we could make everyone think it was real, so it would be convincing. Dom told the agent that everyone would need to know. No secrets."

"Agent Slatter then told Dom that you would be told about the plan and it would be alright. Then when Leo got out or whatever, Lucy could tell him how she did it, get it on tape and then off to jail she goes, right along with Nick," Allie said.

She looked at a stunned Julie.

"Sorry about Nick, by the way. He turned out to be kind of a loser," Allie said innocently.

Julie smiled and chuckled a little. "I know, honey. I'm sorry, too," Julie added.

"At least some good came out of all this. We all know the truth now, and I'm not married to him anymore. He signed the papers that night when he confessed," Julie told her.

"Oh, yeah? That's awesome! I haven't heard about any of that, you'll have to tell me all about it," Allie got side tracked.

"Later, honey," Julie winked, assuring Allie.

"So you knew that night, that you were about to drink

drugged wine and make me think you were dead!" Mark said irritably.

Allie looked her father in the eye, and said "Yes. But, again, you were only supposed to think that for like an hour. Dom tried to get a hold of you as soon as he had permission…-"

"You're missing the point Allie! How could you make that kind of decision without telling me about it? I keep hearing you say, that you're eighteen and it was your idea, but it wasn't your decision to make. You don't seem to fully understand what impact your actions have had on all of us! It was an awfully big gamble for such a little girl to take. I say, shame on the F.B.I, for their lack of professionalism and shame on Dom, for going along with it!" Mark said furiously.

"Your too trusting, Allie! They took advantage of you, and I ought to go kick all their asses for doing it," Mark said angrily.

"I'm not a little girl anymore, Dad. And I'm not as gullible as you think I am. I know that in your eyes, I'm always going to be your innocent little girl… but I have my own good reasons for doing this. I admit that I have made some crazy choices. I'm aware that I gambled on a few things and made a rash decision or two," Allie challenged him.

"You did a little more than make a "rash" decision Allie, you were reckless. You're right, you gambled. You gambled your life just by drinking that wine. Not only that, but you have no idea what I went through, thinking that you died at my expense… because of that… I lost all hope and compassion in this world. I was about to make them all pay the ultimate price for taking you. I was going to kill them, Allie, out of pure hatred and revenge! It was all for nothing really, because of a prank gone wrong," Mark stated.

Williams leaned up against the door and looked down, he couldn't bear to look at Allie right now. He felt the same way Mark did.

"With as much as I despise the man, Nick almost committed suicide because he thought he killed you. Granted it was supposed to be me and he would've danced on my grave, but that's not the point. The point is, I feel like you, Dom and the F.B.I just pulled the cruelest joke on me and I'm not happy about it. Neither is anyone else… they're just too nice to say it, because it all worked out, thank GOD!" Mark exclaimed.

"Not to mention, you were barely an adult when this Agent Slatter talked to you," Mark grimaced. "I can't wait to meet that guy!" Mark growled.

Allie looked over at Julie. Julie averted eye contact with her, and looked down at the floor, same as Williams.

"I'm sorry everybody. I'm sorry for all the pain I've caused. It was never supposed to be a cruel joke or a prank on any of you… just Lucy and Nick. It went all wrong, but I had good intentions. I had my reasons and I have made my bed… I'm prepared to lay in it," Allie said looking up at her dad.

"I take full responsibility for what I did and how I hid it all from you. I know that's what hurts you the most … because that's what hurts me. The next day after I had woken up, I talked a little with Anita. Dom was desperately trying to get Slatter to track you down... but they had their hands full with Lucy and Nick. They said that Dom was NOT allowed to call you, yet. Dom had to wait until they had brought the cops in on it. Anita came into the living room to talk to me. She told me that you had disappeared after they arrested Nick. This worried all of us."

"Dom demanded that Slatter let him call you or at least brief the Captain, but he heard nothing back on the decision until Dom got a call from Lucy. He had to get a lawyer or something to get her out of jail because they needed her to be at the restaurant on time to meet Leo and confess. Finally, Anita came and told me it was time to go and that Dom got permission to call you! The Captain had finally been briefed by the Fed's. Your phone was shut off, so Dom called Detective Williams, who had just left the precinct. Detective Williams met Dom and his F.B.I contact, Agent Slatter, back at the station and they were on their way to find you. They went to Julie's hotel room, but that was a bust. Dom said that you would show up at the restaurant; he just knew you would be there," Allie finished.

Everyone sat in silence, just taking it all in. That was it... no more to know about it. They all knew how it had ended, except Julie.

"Then what happened?" Julie asked curiously.

"I'll explain it to you later, Jules," Mark sat down on the side of the bed and reached out to hug Allie.

"I'm sorry I got upset and raised my voice. I'm so happy that you're alright and I get to have a second chance with you. I love you so much, Allie cat," Mark said tenderly.

"I did it for us, Dad. We don't have to worry about that family anymore. All of our secrets are out and dealt with. We have each other and we have a new life ahead of us... a REAL future that's ours, not a fake one made up by bureaucrats. That was my intention all along," Allie said humbly.

Marked hugged her and kissed the top of her head. "I had no idea that you knew as much as you did. I didn't know that you remembered anything. How come you never talked to me about it before?" Mark asked.

"You never asked," Allie said clearly. "Plus, I didn't want to upset you and ask questions about stuff that we couldn't say anything about, being in witness protection and all. I felt like I couldn't talk to you about anything," Allie explained.

"I'm sorry for that. I should've been more sensitive to your feelings and not pretended that our old life never existed. That was unfair of me to expect that of you. You were just so young, I had no idea that you would even remember," Mark looked at Allie. "You're so smart, honey. You're incredibly brave and I shouldn't have underestimated you or dismissed you as being "just a little girl," Mark said sincerely.

Mark finally understood her logic. He would try to be as open and understanding with her as he could. It would take him some time, but he would make the effort. She was definitely worth it.

"Thanks dad. That means a lot. I hope you're not too disappointed in me," Allie wiped away a tear.

"Angry? A little. Confused? Definitely," He smiled at her. "But disappointed? NEVER! You damn near single handedly created an investigation and brought down Lucy Vanzetti! It was all you baby girl, I couldn't be more proud!" Mark exclaimed.

Williams and Julie laughed and applauded Allie as well.

"We did it together, Dad. Think about it… we worked together and didn't even realize it! All the extra video and audio you got is the reason why they're going away for good! If we could've given you and Williams another couple of days you would've figured everything out. You would have figured out I was alive! I bet you secretly felt it all along," Allie boasted.

Mark thought about it.

"You know… maybe I did. It sure does explain a lot. But it would have been Williams that figured it out. I didn't have the patience for it," Mark chuckled.

"Okay, okay. Besides the whole "blow 'em all away" plan of yours... you did very well, Dad. You still got it, you know!" Allie laughed.

"Wait, what?? What in the world am I missing here?" Julie asked.

Williams burst out laughing. "I would be honored to have you as my partner, any day. I would not want to get on your bad side, "staged set up" or not," Williams smiled.

"I'm ready to get out of this hotel now, that's for sure. Then you guys can tell me what happened at the OK corral," Julie said.

"I'm ready to get out of here, too. What do you say; we stop and grab a burger before heading home?" Mark asked everybody. "I'm freaking starving," Mark stood.

"Sounds like a plan. What do you think, Julie, are you ready to go home?" Allie grinned.

Mark grinned at Julie and she instantly knew what Allie meant by "home."

"Yeah, I'm ready. I'd dig a guacamole bacon burger right about now!" Julie laughed.

"You'd "DIG" it?" Mark laughed.

"Yeah, I would!   Don't make fun of me!" Julie laughed.

"I'm not making fun. I'm never going to get tired of you and all your sayings," Mark said sweetly.

"Come on, Williams. Meet us at the house? I'm buying," Mark picked up Julie's bag.

"No, thank you. You really need to spend time with your family," Williams opened the door for them.

"I hate to tell you man, but your family now. We'll pick you up a burger and take it to my house. You run home and shower and meet up with us there," Mark said smiling, as they made their way out to the parking lot.

"So, now I need a shower? Are you saying I smell?" Williams sniffed his shirt.

Allie and Julie giggled as they walked to the car.

"Hey, you're the one that said it man, not me," Mark smiled. "See you at the house, brother."

Williams nodded at Mark and waved to the girls.

CHAPTER 20

AGENDA

Williams was eating dinner over at Marks place for the second time that first week after the ordeal. Despite Williams claims that they didn't need him there intruding on their family's privacy, Mark quickly dismissed him by saying, "Do I need to go over this again? You're a part of this crazy family now."

After dinner that particular Sunday evening, Mark and Williams were discussing the media and the details of the investigative findings around the dinner table.

"As you know, the F.B.I., as gracious as they are, has put a gag order on everyone, mostly because of the classified information. Albeit, someone might say, it was to save their own asses," Williams took a swig off his beer.

"They might as well release a statement that says, "Please don't tell anyone how badly we screwed up and how we manipulated a young girl and tricked her family to get what we want in the name of JUSTICE.""

Mark laughed. "What? They wouldn't dare do something so ridiculous and self-serving. Why would you imply such a thing? This is our government you're talking about, they wouldn't lie to us," Mark said sarcastically.

"Captain Haddock is restricted on what he can say, but he still managed to comment on "The combined effort of the Police Department and the F.B.I., and that they couldn't comment any further for fear of jeopardizing the case that they worked so hard to solve," Williams smirked.

"That figures. Well, that's just politics, bro. Everyone has to cover up the ugly and come out on top… looking good," Mark laughed.

"Yep, you're right about that," Williams continued.

"I thought it was a bit odd, that the very next day, however…a "leaked story" about a father and daughter, who helped the local authorities with an ongoing investigation, began to surface all over the internet. Basically, headlines like, "Local family aids in secret investigation." to "Young woman risks life to serve the greater good". They're the weeks most searched Hot Topics on the web, you know," Williams stated.

"The articles were quickly followed by, "sources unknown. You wouldn't know anything about that would you?" he smiled slyly.

"I've heard a thing or two about those, too. Allie has had a field day trying to explain things to people...without "really explaining" what has happened. Most people are just as confused as we are... right, honey?" Mark looked at Allie, who had a grin on her face as wide as Texas, metaphorically speaking.

"Oh, yes, absolutely," she agreed. Allie's intrigue was revealed by her twinkling eyes, confirming Mark's suspicion.

"Yep, she leaked it. I wouldn't be surprised if Jen had a hand in that as well," he chuckled.

Allie laughed. "Oh, you crazy investigative types, always looking for what isn't there. Maybe you should've been a journalist!" Allie smiled widely.

Julie playfully rolled her eyes at them, and stood to clear the dishes.

"Let's go see what's good on T.V. Allie-cat. This could take a while," Julie gestured towards the living room.

"What?" Mark and Williams said in unison.

"You know what," Julie pointed at Mark and smiled. "This on-going banter of yours and talks of a conspiracy theory concerning an already closed case," Julie said.

"It's all in good fun," Mark held out his arms playfully.

Julie blew a kiss at Mark.

"Leave the dishes in the sink, Williams and I will get them," Mark leaned over and kissed Allie on the top of her head. Both the girls paused for a moment.

"Go, go, go!" shouted Allie. The girls pretended to bolt from the dining room, gladly accepting his offer.

"Get outta here before he changes his mind!" yelled Allie.

~

"So, how is Julie doing with everything? You guys sure do look happy together," Williams said as he rinsed the salad bowl that Mark just washed.

"She's doing great. She fits in here really well," Mark said smiling.

"She's moved most of her things into the house, while slowly sorting out her legal affairs with Nick. The divorce papers were signed and Nick has surprisingly, stayed true to his word. He gave her practically everything, even though she didn't want any of it," Mark commented.

Williams nodded.

"It's not like he's going to be using any of it any time soon. The charges brought against him, are mounting up... he's looking at a life sentence in the least," Williams added.

"As soon as they had the chance, Lucy and Nick couldn't wait to spill the beans on each other... they even did it without making deals for lesser time, stupid criminals," Williams and Mark chuckled to themselves.

"Whatever happened to "honor amongst thieves?" Williams added.

"With the exception of Nick's personal stuff, Julie has decided to sell everything, including Nick's truck and their home. Nick's sister took his family pictures and put important papers and stuff in storage and let Julie donate the rest. Clothes, furniture, his books, magazines... she just put it all out on the curb and made a call," Mark said.

"That's good, I suppose. Clean slate. I bet she's anxious to put that life behind her," Williams said.

"Yeah, I think so, too. I told her she had all the time in the world to make up her mind... she could stay here or there, if she was more comfortable, but she really just wanted to get it over with and stay with me and Allie. She said it was nothing but a house of lies, and she doesn't ever want to live like that again," Mark said.

Williams nodded. "I could only imagine how difficult that must have been for her to deal with. It's such an awful thing to happen to such a nice girl."

"It's his loss and my gain for sure. For the first couple of days, I kept asking Allie if she was alright with Julie moving in. You know, just trying real hard to include her in the decisions I was making, and every time, Allie would say... "Of course, I want her here silly. Or, "Dad, stop asking, you're going to hurt her feelings if she hears you!"

"I just wanted to make sure she felt good about it too, you know. A lot has happened, really fast," Mark said.

"I understand," Williams nodded.

"Allie surprised me the other night after I had asked this last time and she turned to me and said, "You and Julie being together, seems more logical to me than anything else that has gone on lately. I have always felt that there was something missing here in our home and with Julie being here, it suddenly feels… whole."

"Wow. That's a pretty bold and direct statement," Williams said.

"Yeah, tell me about it. I was so happy to hear that. My daughter never seizes to amaze me. Just when I think I have an idea of how she feels or if I think I know what she's going to say, she just blows me away with how compassionate and incredibly smart she is. She's way more mature than I give her credit for," Mark said honestly.

"Does Allie plan on staying local after high school?" Williams asked. "I always wanted my daughter to stay with me and attend the University here."

"Allie will be graduating High School in the spring and plans on moving out. Allie and Jen have plans on finding a place together and going to the University. Allie thinks Julie moving in is perfect timing, and this way she won't, "feel like she's leaving me all alone."

"That makes sense to me! I wouldn't want to leave you alone either. We all know what happens! You turn into a renegade vigilante!" Williams smiled as he listened to his friend.

Mark laughed. "Ha-ha, very funny. Allie feels like she won't have to worry about me as much and she can feel more confident about her decision to move and be more focused on school."

"That's good," Williams agreed.

Mark continued. "It kind of resonated with me, to hear that my daughter feels so responsible for me and worries about me so much. So, I'm glad that she's going to gain some independence from this." Mark said truthfully. "I just never realized that most of her decisions were based on me and what I wanted or needed."

"Well, she cares about you very much, Mark. I think it's a good thing she's going out into the world. She needs to know you support her. Not that you need my opinion, but I'm glad to hear everything is coming together for all of you. Everything is going to be just fine from here on out," Williams said sincerely.

"Thanks. I appreciate it, bro. I think you're going to be doing pretty well for yourself also," Mark said.

"Speaking of Allie, she seems like she's doing good with the fall-out from her role in the investigation and all," Williams asked.

"Well, despite all the attention she's been getting from the newspapers and numerous reporters wanting her exclusive interview, she's actually doing quite well. She doesn't seem traumatized by it at all. In fact, she thinks it was the coolest thing she has ever been a part of. I told her she's going back to school tomorrow, to get back in the swing of things. I think she's okay, emotionally, so I thought it would be best for her to go right back to school and get back to normal. It's been a week, I think it's been long enough," Mark said.

"I completely agree," Williams added. "That girl has guts, doesn't she? Most girls her age and even older wouldn't have pulled that off. She was very brave."

Suddenly, Allie came into the room to say goodnight to them.

"Am I interrupting the discussion on how cool I am? I could sit over here and wait till you're done," she joked.

"No, you need to get to bed," Mark walked over to her hugging her.

"Now, are you 100% sure that I need to go back to school tomorrow, Dad?" She grinned up at him.

"Yes, I'm definitely sure. There's no getting out of it," Mark said sternly.

"You mean I can't call in dead?" Allie winked.

Williams and Mark laughed.

~

That night, before leaving, Williams told Mark and Julie about his plans to take a REAL vacation, and go visit his daughter in Washington. "It will be a couple of weeks before I get back. I'm hoping that she will want to come here to visit over Christmas break, and be able to meet everyone," Williams said hopefully.

"Oh, that would be wonderful!!" Julie exclaimed as she hugged him.

"Going to spend time with your daughter is awesome, I'm happy for you. It's about time," Mark patted him on the shoulder.

"Thanks guys. So, looks like I'll be doing a lot of shopping over the next couple of weeks and walking the windy beaches getting to know my daughter," Williams said optimistically.

"Oh, she's going to love that, I'm sure," Julie said kindly.

"I think we can manage to stay out of trouble for a couple weeks… at least until you get back," Mark said.

Williams laughed as he stepped outside and they waved goodbye.

~

Mark thought that everyone's lives seemed to be headed in a positive direction, with a newly renowned sense of purpose and drive… except his own. His path seemed blurry in comparison. He felt unsure about his future now, than he ever had. Before this, his focus was always on Allie, working, and burying his painful memories under layers of pent up anger and hidden regret. Now, there was nothing to hide, and Allie was practically grown. Well, almost. Besides his daughter, he had Julie by his side, and that alone gave him the feeling of hope.

Despite how he felt about Dom, Mark would have to return to work sometime. Wouldn't he? After all, it was his job, his livelihood. But Mark sensed that there was more than just a disagreement with Dom, other than how things went down. Now that they knew each other's secrets, it would all be different. Mark wasn't entirely unrealistic, but he didn't expect it to be the same. He had thought about quitting the restaurant all together and going to work at the Police Station. Captain Haddock had called and offered him a job, with Williams putting in a good word for him. He just hadn't called him back. He hadn't returned anyone's calls.

"You know, I think I read somewhere that Angelo's is re-opening this week," Julie mentioned that night. They were sitting up in bed together. Mark was watching a rerun on television, while Julie read a book.

"Oh, yeah, does it say that somewhere in your book? Let me see that," Mark grabbed at her book and pretended to try to read it.

"I don't think so, smart guy!" she joked. "You know where I'm going with this," Julie closed her book and gently smacked his arm with it.

"Why don't you just go down to the restaurant, and tell Dom how you feel? You can base your decision off of how that conversation goes, on whether you can work with him again, or if you even want to stay at the restaurant at all." Julie grabbed his hand and lifted it up and over her head, wrapping it around her, snuggling closer to him.

"You didn't have a problem voicing your opinion at the F.B.I. headquarters, or when dealing with anyone else for that matter," she glanced up at him, and he shrugged his shoulders, not disagreeing.

"Speaking my mind isn't the problem," Mark said.

"I know that. I also know that you're not talking to Dom because you want to avoid him. You're avoiding him, because you're mad that he betrayed your trust. You're mad, because he's your friend and you care about him and hurt feelings are involved."

Marks body felt suddenly rigid. Julie knew she hit a nerve on that one.

"He WAS my friend," Mark corrected her. "He put my daughter in harm's way, to accommodate his own agenda and I won't ever forget that," he said sharply.

Julie sat up now and faced him.

"I understand. I really do, and I know why you feel that way. I respect that, and I know it's your choice to make, and I support you no matter what, but I do think you should talk to him, man to man. You'll feel better," Julie said convincingly. "There. That's all I'm ever going to say about it."

She pretended to zip her lips.

"Good. I was just wondering if you were ever going to shut up," Mark said smiling.

"Hey! You want to fight? I know how it get's you going…" Julie shoved him backwards with both hands. Mark gently grabbed her by the wrists and pulled her close to him.

CHAPTER 21

PRIDE

Mark slowly walked in through the front doors of Angelo's Restaurant. He didn't quite know what to expect, but he was very determined to talk to Dom and hear his explanation. It would not consist of the usual pleasantries, like any old conversation the two of them would've had in the past.

Mark is a confident man and isn't used to feeling this uneasy or uncertain, but walking into the restaurant seemed to comfort him somehow, and take the edge off.

The ambience seemed normal, like any other day. To Mark, it was exhilarating! He had definitely missed this place. The immediate faint smell of the wood polish used in the entry way seemed like a welcome card to his senses. The familiar sounds of food being prepped in the kitchen and old-school Italian music over the stereo system was more than just music to his ears. It was like Italian chicken soup for his soul.

He noticed a couple waitresses that were busying themselves with the silverware and napkins, arranging them at the tables. He politely nodded "good afternoon" to Sophia, who smiled up at him as she organized menus at the Hostess podium. Mark made his way past the bar, where Josh, the bartender was finishing up his inventory. Mark was glad he had hired him because he always had a great attitude, very up-beat and was always smiling.

"Hello, Mr. Anderson! How are you today, sir?" Josh was surprised and glad to see him.

"I'm wonderful, Josh! Thank you. How are you today?" Mark asked.

"Fantastic, Sir, thank you for asking," Josh answered cheerfully.

"Good to hear it, Josh. Have a nice evening tonight," Mark added.

Mark walked through the main dining hall and turned right, heading down the hall towards Dom's office. He stopped and gave himself a moment before knocking.

"Please, come in!" Dom yelled as he looked up from the paperwork at his desk. Mark slowly walked in and closed the door behind him.

"Marko," Dom was truly surprised. "It's good to see you. Please, sit down," Dom stood and gestured in front of him at the empty chair.

"Thank you," Mark sat down and looked at Dom.

Here they were now… face to face.

"How are you?" Dom and Mark asked each other at the same time.

"I'm fine, thank you," Mark answered.

"Good. Good to hear," Dom smiled warmly.

Mark felt surprisingly better about talking to him. He wasn't as angry as he thought he would be.

"I know you've come to discuss many things with me and that's perfectly acceptable, in fact I look forward to it. With all due respect, may I just say something first?" Dom asked.

"Sure, by all means," Mark said.

"First, I would just like to say that I am very glad that you have come to talk and I'm grateful for that," Dom said sincerely.

"I don't expect anything from you and I know I am not deserving of your trust, so regardless of what you say to me, good or bad, I will respect you and your feelings," Dom finished nervously.

Mark felt alarmed. He had never seen Dom act so nervous before. There would have to be a good reason for it in order for Dom to be so outwardly sensitive.

"Thank you for taking the time to meet with me. And you're correct, There are certain things I came here to say," Mark cleared his throat.

Dom gestured with his hand, for Mark to continue.

Mark looked at Dom for a moment and steadied his voice.

He began speaking calmly. "I understand why you couldn't tell me about Allie. I know it would have interfered with the investigation surrounding Lucy. I know now, that you had every intention of telling me, but because of miscommunication with your F.B.I. contact and my lack of availability, that never happened according to plan. With that said, I am still upset that you didn't tell me BEFORE it happened," Mark said adamantly.

Dom listened closely and respectfully nodded in agreement.

Mark fought off his agitation as he thought of what to say next.

"You led me to believe that my daughter had died, Dom." Mark shook his head. "For that I will never truly understand how you could do that to someone, especially a friend, who was supposed to be like family," Mark said bluntly.

Dom opened his mouth to say something and Mark held up his hand to silence him.

"Just listen, please. I'm not finished," Mark said sternly.

"I've had some time to process this whole thing and try to think rationally about why I think you did it. There's a certain part of me that wants to believe that you had nothing but good intentions towards us and you, being an informant, would have to comply with the Fed's rules and demands. I get that part of it, but what I don't get, is WHY? Why do they have you on such a short leash? Do I not deserve to know what they could possibly have on you, to make you be a part of something so deceptive?" Mark asked.

Dom stared at Mark. He was speechless.

Mark could see what appeared to be apprehension in his expression. He was holding something back.

"You're an informant and you did what you had to... for what? What is it? What are the reasons why?" Mark anxiously awaited his answer.

"It's very complicated Marko," Dom said in a hopeless manner.

"Why can't you answer the question, Dom? Do I not deserve an answer?" Mark began to get impatient.

"I mean, how could you do that to me and everyone else and use my daughter as leverage for an F.B.I investigation? You know why I acted the way I did. My family is in witness protection for good reason, which, I'm assuming you knew already... correct?" Mark said sharply.

Dom lowered his eyes for a moment.

"That's correct," Dom said clearly.

"I practically went insane with grief and anger... I could have killed someone... and all for nothing, because it wasn't real. It was a ruse and I was a fool," Mark said finally.

Dom swallowed hard before he spoke again.

"I'll tell you, Marko. I will answer your questions. I will tell you everything you want to know. The truth will be difficult for you to hear, but I will tell you regardless. You're right, you deserve to know. You deserve to know everything," Dom slicked the hair back off his fore head and rubbed his eyes.

Mark patiently waited, anxious to hear what he had to say.

Dom's hands shook as he took out a bottle of wine from his bottom drawer and quickly poured it into a glass that sat on his desk. He drank it immediately. He turned and grabbed another glass from the cabinet behind him. Mark tried to wave off the unspoken offering, but Dom poured him a glass and sat it down in front of him anyway.

"Have a drink with me, Vincenzo," Dom ordered. "You're going to need it, for what you're about to hear."

CHAPTER 22

GUARDIAN

"Please, allow me to begin by simply saying, I am sorry for causing you such pain and anguish. My deepest, most heartfelt apologies go out to you and everyone else that were hurt. I feel so ashamed for hurting you in the process of aiding the Feds in this case. I feel such sorrow and shame, much more, than I am able to express to you now," Dom said sincerely.

"Let me also state, that I will never, under any circumstances, do anything that will harm or compromise your family in any way, ever again. For what it's worth to you, you have my word on that," Dom said honestly.

"Thank you for saying that Dom, it's very much appreciated," Mark said guardedly. "I accept your apology."

Dom placed his hand over his heart and breathed in a sigh of relief.

"Thank you. That's very good. That pleases me very much to hear. I appreciate your forgiving nature in these unfortunate of circumstances," Dom proceeded.

"I'm now going to tell you some things that few people

know. I feel that now is as good a time as any to tell you where I come from and how I came to be here. It will perhaps, answer some of your many questions and shed some light on my involvement with the F.B.I," Dom explained.

Dom took a drink of his wine and continued.

Mark took a sip too. Maybe he was going to need it after all. The fact that Dom had referred to him as Vincenzo hit a nerve. He hadn't been called that in a long time. Dom continued.

"Many years ago, I was a part of a crime family. It was a nicely operated organization, as far as things like that go. Unfortunately, things began to change as they always do and some members and I decided that we wanted to go another way. I personally, as well as a handful of others, didn't like the road that the "family" was headed down. You see, many of us didn't want anything to do with the drug business, but this was not the case for "The Boss". There was too much money in it for him to simply, give it up. He was more inclined to just get rid of us and continue his business relationships the drug dealers. Many close friends and their innocent family members were killed in cold blood, with no honor, or respect to their families. It was a massacre. It was so tragic… I couldn't get over the betrayal and the loss of my own. I was overcome with anger, rage and grief… I went a little crazy, just as you were about to, Marko," Dom spoke clearly and directly looked into Mark's eyes.

"I was not a cold blooded killer and had never been provoked like this before. There was nothing stopping me. I wasn't half as smart or as sharp thinking as you are, Marko. There was nothing anyone could say or do to stop me. I could not see reason. My need for vengeance was blinded to anything else but retaliation," Dom swallowed hard and continued.

"I alone, murdered the men who had handled the hits on these innocents I speak of now and I was subsequently brought in by the F.B.I. a couple of days later. I wouldn't make a deal until they picked up my sister and put her into Witness Protection. They promised safety and protection for her and a clean slate for me in return for my testimony in a court case to bring down "The Boss."

"The way I saw things was, I was a dead man, in or out of prison… it was only a matter of time. I decided I would do it. I would turn "rat". I was quite determined to bring them all down, regardless of what ended up happening to me. The entire crime family had been torn apart already and everything it once stood for had been long ago disintegrated."

Dom's forehead wrinkled. He had a look of pure disgust on his face. "I no longer cared. I felt no loyalty to them, anymore," he said bluntly.

Mark was intrigued by Dom's admission. Part of it seemed vaguely familiar, but then again, Mark was from an Italian/Sicilian family and in New Jersey, the idea of having old mafia ties and connections weren't unheard of. It was common knowledge.

"So you were able to make the deal and go into hiding for yourself after the trial and they obviously brought you here," Mark assumed.

"Yes. I also managed to give up a few drug dealers and took

them down also. That is how I was able to escape jail time. They offered me a life after relocation, but I was only able to bring my sister with me; Anita," Dom said guiltily.

Mark was suddenly sympathetic to Dom's story. "I'm very sorry for the loss of your friends and family. Criminals or not, no one deserves to lose their life."

Mark realized what he had just said. "I'm a hypocrite." He thought to himself. He would have taken life. He would never understand the grey area of a justifiable homicide.

"I'm glad that you were able to save yourself as well," Mark commented.

"Thank you for your kind words, Marko. That leads me to my next "truth" to tell." Dom began to nervously wring his hands in front of him.

Mark sat attentively listening to his old friend's history.

"Do you think it was a coincidence that you and Allie were brought here, to be relocated?" Dom asked.

Mark was taken aback by Dom's question.

"I don't know. I suppose not. Why, were we brought here to be near you, for some reason?" Mark asked, dumbfounded.

"Yes, you were. You were placed here, so I could keep an eye on you. If something were to happen, I would be able to notify the F.B.I," Dom said coolly.

"Why? Are you some kind of F.B.I. bodyguard for the witness protection program?" Mark was confused. "I don't understand what you're getting at."

"No, I'm not exactly like a bodyguard. There is no one else around here, that I am aware of anyway, that has been relocated. I just have "connections" within the Bureau that would enable me to help and support you if you ever needed anything. Basically it was just more convenient in order to look after you and keep you safe," Dom answered.

It began to make sense to Mark now. Dom was the one who had employed him since the first week he arrived. He also promoted him quicker than any other worker.

"Is that why you gave me all the raises and promotions? Did I not deserve it or earn it on my own?" Mark asked bluntly. He suddenly felt offended.

"Of course you deserved it, Marko! You earned everything you got through your many hours of hard work and dedication. I was also very proud of you to have gone back to school to get your business degree. Don't confuse that with what I'm trying to tell you. Please don't insult my intelligence," Dom answered with a straight face.

"Okay, fine. If I wasn't a special circumstance, does the F.B.I. treat everyone like this whose in the program?" Mark asked skeptically.

"No. It was and still is a special circumstance, Marko, in a more delicate type of situation. I need you to understand one more thing, before I explain the reasons why," Dom stated.

Mark leaned back and crossed his arms, waiting for him to explain.

"I want you to try and understand that my duties were pulled in opposite directions with this current ordeal. There was the F.B.I and there was you and Allie. I had to uphold my duties with the Fed's and comply with their regulations, in order to make sure that you and Allie were both safe in the long run. That meant putting my personal feelings for Lucy aside, and focusing on you and at the same time helping the Fed's with their ongoing case involving the "Information Leak" in the witness protection identification case."

"When Allie told me that Agent Slatter had contacted her, I was outraged. I wanted to end it all. I very easily could have lost all credibility and lost all footing in the investigative aspect of the case. I made the decision that only I and no one else, would handle Allie during the investigation, and stay in it to the very end… for that reason alone," Dom said adamantly. "That was for the soul purpose of watching over her."

That explanation surprised Mark. It actually made a lot of sense to him. He finally understood.

"Make no mistake… you and Allie were always my top priority. Whatever professional decision I had to make, revolved around her safety. I had to give up my Lucy and get over that mess very quickly in order to trap her the way we did. It wasn't pretty, but it was necessary. I would do it again in a New York minute to help you. My hope is that we can move past this confusing time and you will accept my apology for the mistakes that were made," Dom said sincerely.

Mark saw anguish in his old friend's eyes. Torment, even.

"Apology accepted. I understand now how difficult it must have been for you, in many different aspects. Thank you for watching over us the way you have, all these years, but there's no reason for it any longer. Allie and I are not of your concern, so please don't think you have to carry that burden any longer," Mark said

"What if I could have kept it all from happening? All of this could have been avoided," Dom quietly asked.

"How could it have been avoided? No one blames you for Lucy, Dom. That was all her. Don't feel guilty for that." Mark said seriously. "That woman is a certifiable whack job, who had us all fooled. It had nothing to do with you at all. That's on Leo… he created that Monster by lying," Mark said frankly.

Dom stared at Mark for a moment, contemplating his next words, carefully.

"I regret not being able to bring you with me in the first place. None of this would have ever happened. Alice would still be alive," Dom said quietly.

Mark was suddenly rattled. "What do you mean by that?" Mark blurted out. He looked at Dom angrily.

"I tried to extend the witness protection deal with the F.B.I. to bring you all back with me. You were all in danger of being killed. I bargained and flipped on many people just to satisfy the agents involved, to bring back Anita. They were sympathetic to my plight, but said it could not be done for you," Dom lowered his eyes in shame.

"Are you talking about my mom and my sister? How does your story have anything to do with my family?" Mark asked frantically.

Dom spoke slowly.

"All these years later, when I found out about what happened to Alice, I was beside myself with guilt. I almost left the program. I wanted to run from the Feds and give it all up out of pure spite. Then they gave me you and Allie. They knew I wouldn't leave or ever entertain the idea of trading there confidences anymore."

"Dom, answer me! How do you know us?" Mark demanded to know.

Dom took a deep breath and collected his courage.

"My given name, is Lorenzo Salvatore Santoro," Dom said clearly.

Mark stared in shock. His body went numb. The hair stood up on the back of his neck, as the tingle of goose bumps spread over his body. He studied Dom's face for a sign of truth. Although it was hard to remember much from his childhood, he would always remember his father's last name.

"Your father, Salvatore, was my oldest brother. I'm your uncle, Vincenzo," His voice began to crack. "You are my blood."

Tears that had welled up in the old man's eyes now flowed willingly. He quickly pulled out a kerchief from the inside of his jacket pocket and began to quickly wipe them away.

"Please, excuse my tears," Dom began to speak, but was caught off guard by the sudden rush of Marks body leaning over the desk to embrace him. Mark didn't care if he cried in front of him, he hugged him tighter.

"I remember you!" Mark cried happily. "You're my Uncle, Enzo!"

CHAPTER 23

THE TIES THAT BIND

Mark strongly felt that in his heart, he knew that Dom was his uncle. He was overcome with emotion. Dom patted him hard on the back, as Mark gave a final squeeze before letting up.

"Uncle, why didn't you tell me sooner?" Mark was bewildered. He sat back into his chair.

"I couldn't reveal my identity, same as you. That's the basic rule of Witness Protection 101," Dom joked.

"I'm not supposed to disclose my identity or blow my cover as being an informant either. I guess I just decided that after these recent events, "To hell with them," Dom laughed.

"It doesn't matter to me anymore, what they think. It was necessary for me to tell you. If they expected me to keep quiet after everything that has happened... then they simply have unreasonable expectations, don't they?" Dom smiled.

Mark laughed. "Oh, my good God, I can't believe this." Mark ran his fingers through his hair, scratching the back of his neck.

"Well, it's nice to see you... if that makes any sense! You look so different than what I remember. I can't believe I didn't figure it out sooner, or at least have an inkling of an idea," Mark studied Dom's face, for the first time it seemed. Mark looked puzzled.

"You were very young the last time I saw you. Maybe, seven years old. No?" Dom guessed.

"Yeah, I think that's about right. I haven't seen you since before my father left," Mark remembered. He took a drink of his wine now and sat back into the chair. He felt strangely lighthearted all of the sudden. It was a nice change in mood for once.

"Well, I guess if I'm still Marko than I'll keep calling you Dom!" Mark chuckled.

"It seems so weird to me right now, to associate you and my Uncle Enzo as the same person," Mark said. He was bursting at the seams. How exciting this was for him, he felt like a little boy again. He couldn't wait to tell Allie about Dom and Anita.

"Anita!" Mark shouted, as he suddenly remembered her. He hadn't put that one together yet. Mark struggled to recall her from his childhood.

"Antonia, my younger sister; she would often baby sit you and even helped your Mama to give birth to Alice," Dom recalled. "We secretly reminisce together on occasion," he smiled slyly.

Mark pointed in the direction of the main dining hall, "And Sophia? She's really my cousin?" Mark was thrilled.

"Yes, she is as a matter of fact. Anita was briefly married, but they divorced when Sophia was very young. I have taken care of her since," Dom added.

"You're my Godfather, aren't you?" Mark grinned.

"It seems I am," He laughed. "That's what it's all about, Marko. Taking care of the family isn't so simple; it entails many things and many obstacles along the way."

His eyes glassed over and his mind seemed to wander. Dom became very serious.

"The truth telling isn't over quite yet, Marko. The rest is basically history, but important none the less. Do you want to hear it?" Dom cautiously asked. His expression seemed to warn Mark.

Mark realized that he had all the answers he needed and more. He was more anxious to put all of this behind him than he ever thought possible. But he couldn't resist. That's just not how he was made. He wanted to know all there was left to know, every last detail.

"Yes, please continue," Mark sat quietly as Dom cleared his throat and situated himself in his chair.

Dom acknowledged this last request and resigned within himself the fate of carrying on with the story.

"I can't allow you to go on in life, thinking that your father left you or abandoned any of you in any way. It is simply not the case," Dom took a deep breathe, and exhaled slowly.

"Your father, Sal, was one of the shot callers in our crime family. He had been quarreling with "The Boss" for months over a difference of opinion. When you add unwanted drug shipments and low life drug dealers in the mix, things get complicated. Your Father didn't want drugs anywhere near his neighborhoods. Although we dealt our share of guns, dappled in gambling and other less than impressive illegalities, he didn't want to be caught selling or distributing such vile, life threatening substances. He felt very strongly about this," Dom glared at Mark, sternly making his point.

Mark nodded. His mind had already begun to put together the scenario, but hoped for a different outcome.

"Sal put it out there on the street, that if he ever saw or heard of a single drug deal go down in his territory... he would kill them on the spot, personally. Many of us felt the same. We supported his decision," Dom said passionately.

"This angered the drug dealers, especially since "The Boss" had already made an agreement with them, a business arrangement of sorts. Sal and I, a good friend of ours from high school named Bobby, stayed true to our beliefs. There was a rift forming in our group and many were afraid to publicly agree with us. We suggested that we part ways, but "The Boss" said it wasn't necessary. He just said he was going to squash the deal and we had nothing to worry about. We were all very skeptical of his sudden change of heart. Sal no longer trusted him."

"So, after a meeting one night with these drug dealers, "The Boss" decided that in order for things to run smoothly and keep his drug business profitable, he needed to get rid of us. "Thin the herd" so to speak," Dom paused and looked at Mark. His heart sank.

"Bobby and his wife were hit first. They were stabbed to death in their car, sitting in their driveway, just coming home from church," Dom closed his eyes as he remembered.

"Oh, my goodness," Mark whispered. Mark had seen plenty of death and murder having been in the war and on the force, but you never get immune to hearing how shockingly cold blooded and sadistic some people can be.

"Senseless," Mark thought. "That's incredibly senseless."

"Sal and I knew we were next. The end of the "family" was apparent and we knew we couldn't trust anybody, but ourselves. Sal took a couple of the most loyal guys and went home to pack you all up and move you out of town. I returned home and found the housekeeper shot to death on the kitchen floor. I went to look for my wife and that's when I discovered she had been gunned down in the bedroom," Dom's hand shook and he cleared his throat.

Mark said nothing, respectfully allowing Dom to finish his painful story.

"The men were coming for me, but I didn't care… but I wanted to make sure you had all gotten to safety. I literally ran seven blocks to your house and found it ransacked. I found no bodies and took it as a sign that you all got out of there in a hurry," Dom said.

Mark vaguely remembered something about that.

"That must've been when we moved to Jersey. We lived in a basement apartment of some old guy's house," Mark struggled to remember. "I remember he was always grumpy and we couldn't go outside to play very often."

Dom smiled a half smile. "He was someone that we had helped in the past. He was indebted to your father and was repaying a favor. He was a good man. Forgive me, I cannot recall his name," Dom said, solemnly.

Mark nodded and felt a pang of guilt. He didn't remember his name either. Mark made a mental note of it. He would find out somehow and pay his respects to the family.

"Sal was able to find me the next day. He said he wanted to go to the F.B.I.! I thought he was crazy... but I understood what he was trying to do. He just wanted you all safe and he was willing to do whatever it took. The Fed's had been watching all of us for quite some time. Constantly contacting us and saying things like, "We already know about everything... we just need specifics. We can protect you; you're not the ones we really want. "

"It was the same ole, "song and dance" speech and we dismissed it every time. But this time was different. Sal was desperate to protect you and the girls. Later that same day, another one of our guys, Frankie, was found in his bath tub beaten to death. His wife and son had been shot in their heads while they slept."

"That's horrible," Mark saw the pain in Dom's eyes as he continued to explain.

"Yes, it was. It was an example of what they would have done to you and your family. Sal was infuriated. He wanted to confront "The Boss". He called him a coward. Sal decided he would no longer hide from such cowardice men. That's when we received word, that "The Boss" wanted a meeting."

"His message was simple. He wanted Sal and no one else. In exchange, no others would be killed or harmed in any way," Dom shook his head.

"Sal accepted, right away, and the meeting was set. I begged Sal not to go. I told him if I went with him, I could protect him. He was walking into certain death and he knew it but he insisted that he go alone, for I would surely be killed as well. He told me who was going to be there, so I would know who was involved in it. We already had our ideas of who the hit men might have been anyway. Sal handed me a thick envelope with an address on the back. He asked me to deliver it for him. I agreed and we said our goodbyes," Dom's eyes glassed over, once again.

Dom stopped talking for a moment and looked at Mark.

"He made the deal with "The Boss" and sacrificed himself to keep his family safe. That was the last time I saw your father. That is the God's honest truth," Dom's chin quivered and he looked away.

Mark sat in silence with Dom for a moment before speaking. He now understood why his mother had changed their last names to Lentini, her maiden name. It was because they were in hiding. It disassociated them from their father's reputation. When his father never returned, he just assumed he had taken off and that it just meant his parents had been divorced. Mark thought it was probably easier for his mother to go with that story, than to tell them he was murdered. The less they knew, the safer they were.

"I'm very sorry that you have had to relive all of that to explain it to me. I appreciate it more than you know. It brings me a little bit of peace actually, knowing what really happened to my father," Mark said sincerely.

"That is why I felt it was so important to tell you, to not only honor your father's memory, but to bring closure for you. Now you can live the rest of your life knowing the truth. He was a good man, who loved you all very much. He didn't want any of you to pay the ultimate price for his career choice. You were all very loved and cherished by him," Dom wiped his brow.

"I understand, thank you," Mark was humbled in knowing the truth now.

Marks curiosity was sparked by something Dom had mentioned. "May I ask you a question?"

"Yes, Marko... anything you like." Dom stood up to stretch.

"The envelope my father gave you... did you deliver it?" Mark asked.

"I did deliver the envelope, but not right away. As I told you earlier, I had some business of my own to attend to," Dom leaned against the desk and looked at Mark, half smiling. "A little "street justice," if you will."

"Do you have any idea what was in it or to whom it was addressed?" Mark asked.

Dom nodded. "It was a letter, I'm assuming. It was addressed to the F.B.I agent that I ended up dealing with. Whatever information it contained, it helped build the case a great deal. I tried to get them to let me find you and the girls to bring you here with me and Anita. You know, to keep us together. Sadly that wasn't a possibility. It wasn't until I heard about Alice, that I found out about your mothers passing. I'm very sorry for your loss it was very tragic. I remember your Mother and Alice very fondly. Allie reminds me so much of both of them," Dom lowered his head.

"Yes, she does, doesn't she," Mark smiled. Mark looked at Dom much differently now. He seemed like he was a completely different person, transformed, right before his eyes.

"May I tell her? About us being related, I mean," Mark asked.

"Oh, of course! As a matter of fact, I would love to be there, when you tell her… and Julie too!" Dom said excitedly.

"That'd be great!" Mark exclaimed. "When would you like to come over?"

"Now is as good a time as any, is that alright with you? Then maybe afterwards, we will all come back here to eat, yes?! What do you say?" Dom asked. He extended his hand and Mark stood to shake it.

"That sounds great, Uncle! I want to thank you again, for all you've done for us over the years. I know my Father would be very proud of you and grateful for what you've been able to do for us," Mark said respectfully.

Dom stood by the door and faced Mark.

"Thank you, Marko. That means a great deal to me. If I could go back and do things differently, so that I never caused you pain, I would do it," Dom said truthfully. "Your Father is looking down on you also and is so proud of the man you have been and of the father you have become. I am so honored to call you my nephew."

Tears stung Marks eyes. He didn't realize until now, how much he needed to hear that. He was overcome with emotion. "I'm also very grateful, to have you back in my life, thank you for saying that, Uncle, it means a lot to me as well," Mark choked back the tears.

"I would like to think, that this means you'll come back to work… and be my partner," Dom held out his hand for Mark to shake. "What do you say, Marko. Can we start our lives over?" Dom asked, trustingly.

Mark looked into Dom's face seemingly, for the first time. He recognized the familiar shape of his nose, the same as his fathers, and of his own.

"Absolutely… Uncle. I look forward to the bright futures of our family and our business," Mark reached out and firmly shook his Uncles hand. The two of them embraced and slapped each other hard on the back, laughing as they walked out into the hallway.

~

Side by side, chatting and laughing with one another, Dom and Mark sauntered through the main dining hall with a renewed sense of purpose and direction in their life. They smiled and acknowledged the waiters and waitresses as they began their dinner service. Sophia seated an older couple and looked up and smiled at them, with understanding in her eyes. Mark graciously nodded and smiled back. The men stopped just short of the entrance and turned around to gaze over the restaurant.

They both knew that from here on out, their business and personal lives would never be the same. Mark, especially, felt inspired and encouraged to embrace his suddenly optimistic future, whatever changes it may bring. Change is after all, a good thing. They would both adapt to these changes just as they had done all their lives. It had been a long, hard road for them both, but now they would create their own destiny's and would no longer hide behind false security. Mark wouldn't have it any other way.

EPILOGUE

ITALIA

The snow drifted softly across the cold, dimly-lit parking lot of Angelo's Restaurant. Glowing lights shown through the frosted windows, illuminating the snow covered shrubs beneath them. Laughter and loud jubilant voices could be heard from the sidewalk. Warm and inviting, it was surreal and magical. It was Christmas Eve.

Almost four months had passed since Allie's fateful birthday party.

Tonight was yet another special dinner for everyone. Although they really didn't need an excuse to get together, each and every one had gathered together tonight to celebrate what they were all thankful for… family.

"Every dinner is like Thanksgiving, in our family," Allie joked.

Detective Williams sat next to his daughter Kate and happily watched as she giggled and talked with Allie and Jen. He was so happy to have her cheerful spirit back in his life. Mark sat back in his chair, looking relaxed as ever. He had his right arm draped loosely around Julie's waist. Julie was leaned forward, deep in discussion with Sophia about a movie they had just seen together.

Mark lightly traced his fingers over her left hand that lay on his knee. Their matching gold wedding bands gleamed brightly in the candle light. Mark allowed his gaze to wonder momentarily away from Julies glowing face to take a moment and glance around the dinner table. Dom's eyes met his.

Dom smiled proudly at Mark as they nodded respectfully at each other. They both silently acknowledged their good fortune. Dom sat at the exact opposite end of the table as Mark, both watching and observing their wonderfully entertaining family. Anita, who sat at Dom's side, stood and began dinging her glass to get everyone's attention.

"Attention! My brother has a wonderful announcement!" Anita said excitedly. She playfully bowed towards Dom and gestured for him to stand.

"You want me to speak right now?" asked Dom.

"Yes, right now!" Anita was extremely anxious for Dom to tell everyone about his surprise he had for them.

"Oh, all right!" Dom slowly stood. "I suppose I could let the feisty cat out of the proverbial bag," he joked.

Mark said loudly, "I don't know about this, Uncle. I can't take too many more of your surprises!" he joked.

"No kidding!" Allie chimed in.

Dom laughed and waved them off. "No, no. This is a good surprise, I promise! It's just a little Christmas gift for all of you," Dom said coyly.

"Little?" Anita scoffed. "Tell them, already! I can't stand it any longer!" she laughed.

"What is it, Uncle?" Sophia asked curiously.

Everyone quieted and looked at up at him, intrigued by Anita's excitement.

Dom began slowly. "I have made arrangements, for everyone at this table..."

Williams and Kate glanced at each other, wondering what could possibly include them as well.

"Everyone, including myself, will be spending Christmas Break, on vacation!" Dom exclaimed.

The girls gasped. Everyone was so surprised and very excited, all except for Mark. He had many questions. He was concerned with the restaurant and wished that Dom would have included him in the planning. Perhaps he could split the cost. He would settle up with him later.

"Dom, are you serious?" Mark tried not to scowl.

"Tell everyone WHERE we're going!" Anita stood and grabbed hold of her brother's arm, excitedly.

"Why don't you do the honors?" Dom indulged her.

"Don't mind if I do! Listen up every body, we're all going to … ITALIA!" she exclaimed.

Williams and Mark gasped now. Julie leaned back and covered her mouth. "Mark!" she whispered excitedly. "I've never been out of Idaho."

The young girls all squealed with delight and began talking about shopping and what to wear. Williams looked at Dom, cautiously.

"Dom, that's very generous of you, but I don't think we can accept," Williams said realistically.

Dom looked at Williams, puzzled.

"Nonsense, Williams. I would be insulted if you declined." Dom responded. "That goes for all of you," he said sternly, looking directly at Mark.

Dom cleared his throat. "Listen carefully, all of you."

Everyone quieted their noisy chatter.

"For a very long time, I wanted nothing more than to look around my dinner table, as I am now and see the faces of my family smiling back at me. Williams and Miss Kate, you are no exception. You are loyal friends and are thought of fondly, with the highest of respect," Dom looked at Williams and said, "Don't take that lightly."

Williams understood and smiled in agreement.

"Jennifer, young lady, there is no need for me to explain this to you, is there?" he smiled sweetly at her. Jen slowly shook her head and smiled back.

"No, sir, thank you," Jen replied.

"You're quite welcome, young lady," Dom responded. He now addressed the table.

"Now, I would like to take my family to the country in which my father was born and show you the city in which your family comes from. I still have living relatives in the region. It's my greatest wish to introduce you," Dom's voice shook for a moment, exposing his vulnerability.

Dom's family sat quietly and listened to him. They all admired the unconditional love and generosity that poured from this kind and humble man's heart.

Mark thought about it for a moment and no longer thought of the monetary cost involved. He just saw it for what it was. It was a selfless act of kindness that meant so much more to his Uncle, than expenses and work schedules. It was about togetherness and understanding of family roots. That was definitely worth more to Dom, than any amount of money in the world. Everyone, absentmindedly looked to Mark for an answer.

"Okay," Mark said loudly. He smiled at Dom and nodded approvingly at a shocked Williams. "To Italy, we go!"

The younger girls shrieked to each other, excitedly. Julie looked worried suddenly and whispered inaudibly to Mark.

Dom gleefully raised his glass for a toast. "Alright then, it is settled. We have a wonderful trip to look forward to!"

The others raised their glasses as well.

"Hold on to that toast for just a moment," Mark interrupted. "Go ahead, Jules… tell them," Mark smiled a sly grin at her.

"Maybe we should wait, Mark," Julie whispered, shyly. Mark reassuringly kissed her hand.

"Julie's going to tell you about someone else that will be coming along on our trip," he encouraged her.

Everyone looked around at each other, slightly intrigued by who this might be.

Julie swallowed hard and stood up slowly. She had no idea how to begin. "Okay," she said reluctantly.

She took away the thick cloth napkin from her lap that she had gathered and bunched all evening. She straightened her back and squared her shoulders, preparing to speak. She had no idea how to say what she needed to, so she decided to just show them.

She turned to the side and arched her back slightly, gently sliding her hand down over her rounded belly. The stretchy cotton fabric of her dress tightened and shifted revealing her surprise.

"It's still a little early, but we're pretty sure, judging by the 17th week ultrasound photos we got yesterday, that….. It's a Boy!" Julie exclaimed.

The girls reacted first and cried out in joy. Everyone clapped.

Dom began to cry. "Thank you, Jesus!" he praised. He began saying a Catholic prayer in Italian.

Anita went to them at once and began hugging her and congratulating Mark and Julie.

Mark stood up as Dom and Williams came to congratulate and hug him as well.

"I knew it!" Allie said. She raised her hands up in the air as if she were finally being vindicated. "I knew it, I knew it!" Allie grinned wide enough for the whole world to know how happy she was to be a big sister.

Kate, Sophia, Jen, Allie and Anita pulled their chairs over to Julie's and began asking twenty questions. "When did you find out?" Jen asked.

"Can we see the pictures?" Anita asked.

"Well, actually, Mark knew before I did," Julie smiled up at Mark as he stood at the opposite end of the table with Dom and Williams. "The pictures are in my purse, wherever that is…" Julie began to search for her purse, but the girls located it quickly for her.

"Congratulations are in order, brother," Williams shook Marks hand and hugged him, giving him an extra hard slap on the back.

"Thank you! I'm very blessed and extremely excited about him!" Mark grinned.

"It's about time… we need another man around here," Dom joked.

"Forgive me for saying this, but you must have been trying right off the bat, especially if you knew she was pregnant before she did," Williams commented.

Mark's voice became softer. "Well, we weren't exactly trying, but I can tell you, without a doubt, that I know exactly when we conceived and I knew it would be a boy," Mark took a sip off of his drink.

Williams raised his eyebrows. "Say no more, bro," he joked.

"Marko," Dom playfully scorned him. "It isn't respectful to a woman, to "kiss and tell" haven't you learned this yet?" he chuckled.

"Yeah, Mark, don't you know anything about girls?" Williams laughed.

"Your right, Uncle, I know this. I apologize… but when you know, you just know," Mark laughingly looked at Julie now, who looked up at him from across the table, lovingly… knowingly.